HIS BLOODED

MATE

A DARK IMMORTALS BOOK

ELISE WHYLES

ISBN: 978-1-990536-32-8

DEDICATION

To those who have supported me – laughed with
me, cried with me and ultimately have given me a swift
kick in the rear. This one's for you .

ACKNOWLEDGMENTS

Within these pages there are terms, slang, and words which may appear to be misspelled. Please note that in creating the world I took some creative licensing on spelling and so words that may appear to be incorrect are not. Thank you.

Author's Note

Welcome to Dreken, realm of the Vampire Nations. Take care you are not spotted by Saltar's forces – or worse, by the False Goddess of Immortals.

After the slaughter of his wife and driven by grief and rage, Vampire King Hemat condemns all who are associated with his fallen general to a horrifying fate. But evil doesn't rest. Saltar will rise again. The twisted whims of a petty goddess and an undying hunger draw the fallen general from his prison. With his rise, he vows he will burn the vampire realm to the ground to get the throne - and his revenge.

War calls to those who would see freedom reign, even if it means putting aside old grievances and rivalries. Those Hemat condemned and cast aside will join forces to save Dreken and the Vampire nation, but at what cost?

.

Chapter One

210 AD

Shadows slithered across the floor, cutting through the weak flicker of light beneath her door. Bede pulled her knees to her chest, her heart thundering beneath her ribs. She turned, her gaze landing on the tiny figure curled beneath a thin blanket.

Little Una suffered so unnecessarily. Small and delicate, she could not do the arduous tasks their uncle expected of them. Many nights she'd gone to bed hungry, Bede taking the beating her uncle would normally have given her. Her heart aching, Bede stashed another crust of bread and cheese in the crack by her bed. She glanced around at their small, dingy room, her heart sinking. She would rather starve than let her sister go without.

The Roman soldiers who had passed by two days before had taken what little they had to spare. Bede shuddered, the memory of the men's stares upon her enough to turn her empty stomach. When would their suffering ease?

"Momma, Pappa," Bede closed her eyes, a lone tear tracing down her cheek. "'Tis a nightmare we live in. If there is any favor among the gods, they will see us from this misery."

"They pay no mind to us mortals." Una's voice shattered the illusion of her being asleep. "'Tis always been such. Rest, sister, our time here grows short."

Tossing the covers aside, Bede rolled over and dropped to her knees, by her sister's bed. A faint flicker of hope lifted the weight from her shoulders. Perhaps the gods had paid heed to her pleas and would ease their suffering by granting death. "Una, I'm so sorry I woke you."

Unawrapped her small fingers around Bede's hand. "You did not wake me. There is always dark before light, sister, and it's very late for us. There are things in motion we cannot halt. Danger lurks beyond the door."

The icy, monotone of her younger sister's voice left her hollow. Una's words were heavy with warning and Bede was no fool. She trusted her sister's gift – even if others feared it. Her stomach dropped to her feet and Bede swallowed. Who or what was about to spring upon them? Their uncle was twisted, his soul an empty vessel filled with wine and gold. What sort of deal would he make to ensure a visitor paid them a call at such an hour?

Beyond her chamber door, feet shuffled, the harsh grunts of their uncle's breathing whispered through the cracks in the door. The clatter of broken pottery preceded the creak of a door and she winced at the slurred curses spewing from his lips.

A foul mood could only mean a day of misery and little rest come the morning light. If only she were strong enough to take Una and flee.

The clatter of hooves and wheels squeezed through the cracks in the wall. Bede straightened, her heart thundering beneath her ribs. Who would come so late? They hadn't had any visitors since the passing of their parents.

A chill crept along her spine. From beyond the door someone jumped down, harsh breathing competed with the loud belch of her uncle.

"'Tis later than you'd said you'd be here. Well past the hour." Her uncle's angry snarl caused her to shrink back, the hair on her arms standing up.

"Couldn't be he'ped. Done got one of me brood down with the fever."

"Well, got one to replace it. By the gods, I got two. You bring me gold? As right pretty as this one be, you'll easily make the coins back in a night."

"I'd see the merchandise first."

"I told ye, she's a fair girl to look upon. And untouched by any man. Not that I wasn't tempted, but as you know, untouched fetches a fair bit more. Alway someone willing to drop a few extra bits of coin for the pleasure of breakin' one in."

"Fair or no' I'll not be parting from my gold without first seein'. Yer eyes are as sound as the boil on me arse."

Bede shuddered with each approaching footstep. The wall prevented her from moving back any further. Thunder echoed in her head and her throat tightened. Blood rushed from her head, the room spinning. Clenching her fists, breathing steadily, she would be ready.

Gods, be merciful. If that bastard had sold Una, he would pay with his life.

Ice formed in her veins, until it closed around her throat. Her heart pounding against her ribs, an oppressive rhythm that choked her. She shoved the blankets back and rose to face their thin chamber door. Bede bent down, sliding her hand under the edge of the thin sleeping pad and closed her fingers around the hilt of her dagger.

The weight of the blade in her palm was welcomed and she flexed her fingers around it. By the gods, it was the one thing their uncle hadn't sold - because he hadn't found it yet. Greed drove the monster.

Bitterness coated her tongue and her stomach lurched, the hot wash of acrid bile in her mouth barely choked back. when the door swung inward to reveal her uncle's frame. Beyond him another man stood cloaked in shadows. Inwardly cringing at the stench brought by their entry, Bede raised her chin and glared at him. Bede forced a careful mask over her features, a calm settling over her like a well worn cloak. Fear garnered her and her sister nothing, only empowered the man who had betrayed them. If only the gods hadn't been so fickle and cruel, but they were. Una and her would simply need to learn to survive in a new world.

"'Tis late for company, wouldn't you think?" Bede caught the lust flash in both men's eyes as they appraised her and tightened her grip on her weapon. Even the heavy layers of leather and wool she wore did nothing to protect her from their gazes.

He waved the man forward and turned to the man at his side. "A good investment, Lugthor. Many would pay handsomely for such prizes."

"Indeed. And both are still intact?"

"It was a chore but I restrained myself. Ye will be able to auction that off for a right pretty bit of gold."

The words sank like barbs into Bede's soul, her blood boiling, she clenched her jaw together. She would cut out his heart for even dare to think of such things for her sister. The meager contents of her stomach lurched upward and she struggled to keep from throwing up. To be spoken about in such a crude manner, as if she were no more than a beast of burden. She cast a glance between the two men, the lust in their eyes chilled her to the bone. Shuddering, Bede grabbed the blanket and wrapped it around her body. "Get out." Turning to her uncle, she shook her head. "And you would do well to remember this is not your—"

"By the gods, I'd be broke in a day with that sharp tongue. What of that one? That frail-looking one—be good for a bit of entertainment." Lugthor laughed, his gnarled, filthy finger pointing behind Bede.

"Two coins extra and you can have 'em both."

Bede stepped between the stranger and her sister, fury lashing at her with each passing second. "Don't touch her."

"Bede?" Una's scared whisper echoed in her ears. "What is going on?"

"Get dressed, you worthless little shit." The furious snarl filled the small room.

Glaring at the drunken figure looming in the door, she reached for Una's hand. "It will be okay, Una," Bede soothed her, swallowing against her own fear. "Come now, quickly. Dress warmly, sister, we're leaving."

"Leaving? But Momma…"

"She will know us in the next life, my dearest. Come now. It would appear the promise of gold has seduced our kin. They have sold us." Bede sneered. Her hand tightened on her dagger she pressed against her thigh. Before they left the filthy little shack, the man would die. She looked over her shoulder, eyes narrowed and lifted her hand to draw a line across her throat.

Fear darted across their uncle's weathered face before he scurried back out of their room. "Momma's spirit will know where to find us." *Just as she will know who to condemn when the time comes.* Bede offered her sister a weak, strained smile. "I will protect you, I swear on my life. No matter what comes our way, we will survive."

"It is a false promise you offer, Bede." Una huddled on the bed, her blankets wrapped around her, fear in her pale eyes.

"Come, think of this as one more adventure, Una. I promise no harm shall come to you."

"I do not fear for me," A tear spilled over and raced down the pudgy curve of her cheek. "His heart is black, Bede. Blacker than a grave he is, his heart has no emotion but greed. He desires you and will not be swayed to kindness or gentleness."

Bede sucked in a breath at her sister's stark words. She had no doubts Una's words were true, the young girl's visions had never been wrong. Some would consider it a blessing, but for her sister it was no more than a curse. Her heart cracked, pain pouring from the unseen wound. Bede swallowed and pressed her forehead to her sister's. "Dark heart or not, he is a man. He must sleep, and when he does, we will make good our escape. Now, quick as you can, dress and we shall leave this place." Bede's voice wavered slightly. "If the gods will grant us favor we will be well free of the shackles and lash he would have us destined for."

Una offered a weak smile and reached for the thin, worn garment. Wordlessly, they dressed, Bede slid the long, thin blade of her mother's into the scabbard she tucked down the front of her dress. She'd not be some man's toy—no matter the gold that had changed hands tonight.

"Getch'rselves out here. Wastin' time is what you be doing." Bede narrowed her eyes, a shudder racing over her at the fury in the drunken slurs. They'd be well off away from here.

"He grows impatient, Bede. Fearful Lugthore will withdraw offer." Una's small voice held a sad note.

"He is ruled by drink, Una. Come, our future stretches out before us and I would have us far from this place by the rising of the sun."

Wrapping a blanket around Una, Bede tugged her shawl over her shoulders and opened the door. Ignoring the chortling figure of their uncle hunched over a sack of gold and an amphora of drink, she turned to stride toward the door, Una's hand clutched in hers. The sudden appearance of a fat, dirty arm across her path did little but stir the nausea.

"You'd best curb any tricks. I ain't as understanding as the drunken bastard inside is."

"Have no fear, you fat, foul, little creature, any tricks I may have you'll not survive." Shoving his arm from the doorjamb, she pulled her sister out into the night only to swallow a cry. A tired bag of bones dozed in his harness attached to a crude wagon. Six dirty faces peered from the bars, their eyes filled with a mixture of fear, loathing, and sadness.

"Getch'rself into me wagon." Lugthore ran a hand down her back and slapped her ass. "I would be well on the road."

Bede gagged and stumbled forward, her hand tightening on Una's as they moved toward the wagon. The rear door swung open and their new 'owner' shoved her toward it.

"Just to be sure you don't get no ideas," he ground out. "I've two dogs ain't eaten in a day— you or that runt run and I'll let 'em loose on you."

Bede met his stare. "Running is the last thing we will do." Ice dripped from her voice. She lifted her sister into the back and climbed in. Settling on the straw, she looked over those in the wagon. None of the girls even looked at them, the soft sounds of sobs filled the silence. One girl pulled her knees to her chest and rested her forehead on them.

For Una, and for those in the cramped, rancid wagon, Bede would see their bonds broken. Bede leaned back with Una tucked against her side and let the rocking motion of the wagon lull her into a light doze.

~*~

The glide of leather against wood penetrated the silence. Across the room, a floorboard creaked in protest and Gawain straightened in his chair. A swift click and the door of his cottage swung open, the cool night air sweeping into the room. Across the mantle the candles flickered, flames bending as if guided by an invisible hand. The wooden cup of wine spun across the tabletop as Gawain straightened. A low growl escaped as Gawain twisted in his seat and glared over his shoulder.

Dressed in a long coat, his eyes glowing in the shadows, a figure stepped inside and kicked the door closed. He strode forward into the light, his long hair pulled away from his face with a thin piece of leather. Across his chest the familiar emblem of the king was carved into the metal of his armor.

"Fuck the gods." Gawain hissed. His uninvited guest was as welcome as a cup of dead blood. "What brings you to my home, Dorstan?" Gawain eyed the other man with a sneer. He bared his fangs at him and reached for the dagger atop the table, sliding it across the wood.

"The king is not here for you to twist his ear and see me even further from my duties at court. Or have you arrived to taunt me for mistakes made in my youth?" Gawain sighed, he didn't miss the debauchery and games being at court required. Nay, his only regret was being shuffled off like some common whelp the king had deemed worthless.

"Your task has been set." Dorstan huffed and shook his head. "One that is far above your place."

"See to the task yourself then. I've no desire to dance to your tune, lizard-blood."

"As usual, you forget yourself in the presence of a higher ranking–"

"I forget nothing." Gawain snapped his teeth, the tips of his fangs sinking into his bottom lip. "You bait me with your foul stench in my home."

With a leather-encased hand, Dorstan reached into the pocket of his cloak. With a flick of his wrist, he tossed a small bag on the table. "Payment for the gatekeeper as per King Hema's orders. You're to go to the hills of Tara and return to our king with the one who can read souls. 'Tis said she can see beyond the soul, she knows what your end is as it was written long before your birth. I have heard she is of mortal flesh, so Hemat thinks her to be one of the gods' bastards. Do it and you will earn his reward. Perhaps your station can be won back. "

"I've no desire to go about to find some witch." Gawain shoved the coin aside, his eyes never leaving Dorstan's impatient frame.

"'Tisn't a witch you're to seek out." Dorstan smirked, his dark eyes flashing momentarily. "I consulted with several of the sorceresses and Priestess Veronique, 'tis one of the old lines."

"If they be of the old lines then they are hardly worth note. Condemned for the actions of Saltar, as so many were. Hemat will not welcome her. He seeks only to torment the child, if that is the case."

"It is not for you to decide, Gawain. Leave tonight. Take care, the one you seek is hardly more than a babe and sacred to the king. Harm should not befall the creature. 'Tis rumored she is connected to his late and most beloved queen."

A shudder traced over Gawain. Queen Maudhnait, though long-dead, had been revered by Vampire and Dragon alike. As beautiful as she was kind, it had been a heavy blow when she was murdered. Even now, centuries after her death, her name was whispered so as not to anger their king. He still raged at her murder, threatening all who turned from the laws of their kind. To even consider embracing anything beyond the vampire way of life was to risk his wrath—and it could be and often was rather intense.

Centuries had passed since the horrid night, and Gawain loathed each passing year and the renewed grief Hemat was consumed by.

Idly, Gawain traced along the jagged scar that ran the length of his face. Hatred, old and deep stirred within his chest. Although he, like all immortals, had the ability to do so, he refused to heal the wound completely. It was a mark of his failure, of his oath, and until he'd righted his error he'd wear it.

"Pity then. She will remain where she is." Gawain turned away from Dorstan. "I do not hunt women, children…or those who share the blood of a traitor."

"Perhaps if you had not been so slow, so weak, she would yet walk among us. Still, there is no use in lingering on a mistake. The king has spoken, and you will not disobey. You will hunt the child, and you will deliver her to King Hemat as he commands."

Gawain heaved a breath as the door slammed shut, leaving him alone in the silence. He hated the traitors who were whispered about in the shadows. Hated everything they stood for—followers of a traitor, killers, they were lower than low, monsters without a soul. Being sent to bring one back was enough to turn the wine he'd been drinking.

"Surely you don't think you're much different." Seductive, the voice filled his small room before a tall, beautiful woman appeared. Her abundant breasts spilled from the sheer fabric of her gown, and a crown sat atop her multi-colored hair. "Come, Gawain, even you can't be so blind." Her dark gaze trailed over him like a physical caress, lust in her eyes. Her tongue slid out to trace her full, pink lips.

"Blind? You mistake me for another. I have no interest in hearing your drivel."

"Tsk tsk, sadly you have not learned much. But you are young." She licked her lips, hunger in her gaze. "So very young."

"Goddess, leave me in peace. I'm busy." He snarled, rising to his feet. Hemat had ordered him to find the child, he would do so. Success or failure meant nothing, his king would not care. He had not cared in all the years since Maudhnait's death. To enter the mortal realm would take skill. He would need to find a keeper that could locate the child.

"Yes, I can see how busy you are." She trailed a hand along the table as she walked over to him. She paused in front of him and lifted her hand, her long nails scratched through the stubble on his jaw. "Mark my words, vampire. The one you seek will enlighten you. She is sweet, her blood will tease your senses. Better than an aged wine even. The child is not all you will find."

"Why do the gods feel they can just intrude upon people? You were not invited into my home–"

"Or your bed." She giggled and leaned forward, licking along his jaw. Her hot tongue painted the flesh with a scalding trail and Gawain pulled away from her.

"You can't be so foolhardy as to believe Saltar will remain in his prison. Hemat was a fool not to kill him, even now he rattles the bars. Saltar grows stronger with each passing moment. One day he will break free. If he does, he will rise like a plague upon this world. All of the worlds. Dragon, fae, vampire - all will fall to the bitter flames of his rage and hatred."

She leaned forward, her sharp teeth nipped at his earlobe, drawing a drop of blood. She sucked the lobe into her mouth, her tongue swirling around it. Her fingers dipped beneath the collar of his shirt, tracing over his flesh. Her other hand slid around his chest, drifting down his body, to the waistband of his trews where it slid under the leather placket.

"I am not Dorstan, or one of your many toys." Gawain slapped her hand away. "I hold no desire to bed you." Gawain stepped back, a low growl rippling through the room. He reached around her to pull his sword down.

Memory danced like fog through his mind as he turned to stare at the beauty before him. He'd seen her with Saltar, their embrace more than simply friendly. He'd always assumed Saltar was bedding the conniving witch, but he'd been unable to prove it. The goddess had managed to hide the truth quite well, and he'd had nothing to take to his king. Hemat wouldn't have listened anyway, not then.

"I've forgotten nothing. Least of all how dearly you enjoy meddling. Stick to seducing other wayward men, I've no desire to sample what you so willingly sell. If you're truly desperate for a bed to crawl into, I believe your lover is locked within the caverns. You can simply materialize there and slither over him before you taint the rest of the world with the filth between those thighs. I've a portal to catch."

"So quick to war, 'tis a wonder how your species has continued for so many centuries. Make war or love—you will always choose war. How typical of such a bloodthirsty breed, so ready to rush in and lap at the bloodshed. Quite nauseating, really. Be wary, my stout warrior," she purred. "What awaits you is not so easily dismissed as the wind. In fact, what waits you could very well do you in forever."

"I never worry about what awaits me. Danger lies only in the shadows of your black heart. Unlike some of my brethren, I've not taken to believing the lies you spout. Their falsities are limitless and deadly to the unthinking male. 'Tis my task to take care, and I watch my back very closely, especially around you. And unlike others, I'm not so foolhardy as to fall for the pleasures between a woman's thighs. Especially yours." Gawain sneered, raking a hard, disgusted look over her ample curves. His lips turned upward, revealing a fang before he schooled his features into an unreadable mask.

"You know nothing of the pleasures of a bedroom. Taking such a vow makes you still a boy, hardly worthy of note for one such as myself." Amuliana sniffed. "As much as I may like what you have between your legs, I'd rather not tutor you in the fine art of lovemaking. I prefer one with a bit more experience. A bit more talent in the bedchamber."

"Ah you have so much to teach. Pity that those with an honest heart and desire to remain pure have no desire to learn. Be gone from my home, witch, else I forget myself and simply slide my blade through you. I've no desire to taint it with the disease and filth you offer. If you don't mind, I've a task to do and I've no more time to listen to your crooked tongue."

"Indeed, take the utmost care. If your fallen general rises, I am not the only being to suffer. If it bears life, he will slaughter it."

"If he rises it will be on your head. Your interference is solely responsible for the loosening of his chains. Only you would dare to give him a taste of the freedom he craves. But what can one expect from one who lives by the whims of their need for sex? Aye, should he rise it will be on your head and no other." Gawain slammed the door on the eerie cackle of her laughter. Closing his eyes, he exhaled, the air around him wavering before he vanished.

Chapter Two

Thick fog crawled along the ground, wrapping its tentacles around Gawain's ankles. An eerie reddish glow filled the night, casting shadows along the narrow, debris cluttered pathway. Tiny stabbing prickles like splinters pierced Gawain's body as he approached the glowing arch. At his side an older man stood, both hands clutching a gnarled staff, his cloak covering him from head to foot.

"Time grows short, my lord vampire. 'Tis as close as I can get you to the child. Mortals are a flighty group and to see you step through will only stir panic. Take heed, there is danger nearby so be careful." He held out a trembling hand in a wordless request. "Humans are foolish, instinctual creatures who think highly of their prowess. The hunted think themselves the hunter. Rather fanciful if you ask me, they are little more than food."

"Thank you, Gatekeeper." Gawain pressed two coins into the outstretched hand. "I appreciate your service in opening the portal." Adjusting his cloak around his shoulders, Gawain stepped into the bluish light. A thousand fingers clutched at him, dragging him forward with each passing beat of his heart. As he passed through the light the tugging sensation faded to be replaced by a force at his back, pushing and prodding him through the gateway.

Gawain took the final step, the sting of the gateway fading as he passed into the mortal world. Rich, earthy, the smell of moss and freshwater rose around him, blending into the sweet aroma of the thick, lush grass beneath his feet.

He sucked in a quick breath, the stench of something dark and bitter clogging his senses. Beneath it, sharp in its sour notes another odor swirled around him, twisting his gut. The meager meal he'd had before leaving curdled in his gut and he swallowed hard. His fangs lengthened, pressing against his lips.

A shift in the wind carried something sweeter, something he almost recognized. It washed over his tongue, teasing his appetites. His blood heated, rushing through his veins. Sparks danced across his nerve endings, settling in a tangled, tumbling mass in his groin.

She was near.

His body stirred, his cock twitched and stirred to life in a way he'd long denied himself. Gawain flexed his fingers before he tightened his grip on the hilt of his sword, the desire to do battle clawing at his control.

Gawain strode past several boulders and ducked beneath the witch's beard hanging from a thick, heavy branch. Straightening, he swept the small cramped clearing with narrowed eyes. Massive boulders protruded from the earth with deep jagged marks which traced over faint shapes, symbols of ancient times. Thick, moist moss crept across the ground, over the rocks, embracing them like a blanket. A heavy fog rolled along the ground, over his feet, his ankles, swirling and dancing in the night with a silent warning of things to come.

He shivered at the ancient wheeze of the wind blowing along his flesh. The chill crept beneath the leather of his cloak and tunic, to the flesh hidden by his clothes, caressing like an old friend—or a lover. Remaining perfectly still, he listened to the air, the crackle of it gathering and swirling before exploding in a shower of dust. It was time.

Darkness filled the space, the cool night air a relief as he stepped forward. He tensed at the shrill scream of a child behind him ripped through the fabric of time and sent his rage racing over him.

His sword in hand, Gawain whirled on one heel and stalked into the darkness of the woods. Through the trees a small fire flickered and danced in its pit. Hounds snarled and barked, chains rattled. Several frail bodies were huddled beneath the rocking wagon, their hands bound to the underside of the box. The rickety cage on the back trembled and shook, screams of pain and rage filling the night. Grunts of pain and muted curses told of a struggle as the screams grew louder, the sound of flesh connecting with flesh deafening to him. The frail-looking horse nickered in fear. Dogs appeared from beneath the wagon, growling and snarling at him. With a low roar, he sent the dogs cowering under the rickety cart.

The urge to kill lengthened his fangs. Venom dripped from the tips, the taste of blood on his tongue. He swung his weapon easily, his eyes focused on the lumbering figure pulling a small, delicate girl from the back of the wagon. An older girl, her hair in disarray, her clothes ripped and torn, fought with the man. Her nails raked over his flesh, digging furrows that ran red with blood. Rage and fear filled her face.

Fury lashed at him as the brute swung, slamming her to the ground. Blood flowed down her chin, the scent sweet, intoxicating. The woman gathered herself and scrambled to her feet, launching every ounce of her weight at the man's back. A dagger in one hand, her fingers tangled in his hair, she swung wildly.

"Nay, you'll not touch her!" Her voice shook with tears and emotion as she fought. "Damn the gods, you will not lay a hand on her."

Teleporting to the figure, Gawain yanked the woman off the man's back with one hand and thrust his sword with the other. The sharp blade sunk deep into the man's fat flesh. The grate of steel on bone shivered up the blade, through the hilt to his hand. With each shift of the blade he felt the bones give, the flesh yield.

The stench of blood and fat filled the air. It oozed over the blade, staining the slaver's already filthy clothes as it pooled beneath his feet. Blood frothed and gurgled from the man's lips, spattering across the girl's face, her pale hair already streaked with it. Gawain jerked the blade free, balancing it in his palm, and raised it for a killing blow.

His prey spun, massive fists rising to terrorize his assailant. His eyes widened in horror. Color oozed from his face. The throbbing of his blood beneath his flesh was loud in the night air. Gawain narrowed his eyes and bared his teeth, a sneer twisting his lips when the man shrank away from him. The human's rounded body shook as he stumbled backward. Gawain's booted feet took him closer and closer with each stride. He coughed, gagging at the sourness of the man's fear mixed with bodily waste.

"Frails are not to be toyed with," Gawain ground out and grabbed the girl, spinning her away, his sword at the ready as the man heaved upward, a dagger clutched in his hand. Gawain's sword rested easy on his palm, ready, the surface slicked with blood as he faced the coward.

"She's mine to do with as I choose." He gurgled, collapsing to the ground, his weapon falling from pudgy fingers. "Paid ten pieces of gold for 'em both, and I aim to get a might of use out 'em."

Choking back the bile rising to burn his throat, Gawain shook his head. Pathetic. Perhaps he was related in some way to Saltar. "Now she's mine," Gawain declared. Raising his sword, he drove it through the man's chest, pinning his twitching frame to the ground.

He stepped back, his gaze sweeping the clearing. Males such as this did not travel alone, his cohorts would be close. He'd need to find and kill them...

Searing pain lanced through him, splitting his chest. Gawain glanced down. The thin, sharp tip of a blade stuck from his chest. He touched the blade and snarled. The metal was warm, when it should have been cold. Shock slammed into him as a faint pinks glow surrounded the slender blade until it turned a searing red. The blade flashed and the light faded, leaving the blade in its normal state, or as normal as it could be with blood racing down the weapon.

Whirling, his hand already scrabbling for the dagger's hilt in his back, he grabbed his assailant by the throat and lifted. Grunting as he pulled the weapon free, his lips curled upward. "You'd do well, wench, to know your place."

"If you think I mean to let you do her harm…" Sputtering, her nails digging into his wrists, the girl's brown eyes stared into his. Fear lay within the depths but something else stirred. Something dark, dangerous, easily recognized if one knew what they were looking for.

He shifted his grip, loosening his fingers as he pulled her against him. Inhaling, he caught the faint scent of blood, fear, sweat, fire, and something sultry, sweet, and light on his tongue. Drawing the scent deep, he wallowed in it, his body responding to the aroma he'd dreamed of but never found.

Gawain inhaled slowly, his muscles tightening, burning. Using the tip of her dagger, he pushed the material of her shift aside. Pale flesh covered her delicate collar bone, the long graceful line of her throat flowed into narrow shoulders. The scrolling marks of a serpent flared before his eyes. It coiled and danced beneath the girl's flesh.

"Shit!" Pulling her close enough to feel the pebbled hardness of her nipples, he tilted his head. "Your mortal flesh holds no interest for me, my dear. If it be mortal." He swallowed around the lump in his throat, belittling his declaration. His interest stirred, pooling in his blood with hot, heavy intent. For the first time in his life he felt the stirring in his loins, the threat to his vows real. Shaken, he stared at the girl, his mind racing as he wondered what it all meant. Suddenly, the gatekeeper's words came back to him, and he shuddered; was this the one he was to watch out for—the one who would guide him to his future?

"Let her go, she meant no harm." Tiny hands pulled on his sleeves. "She sought only to protect me. Please, I beg of you, let her go."

Irritation flared at the dart of heat in the girl's eyes with the other's struggles. Ignoring her, Gawain turned to stare into the wide, startled gaze of a young girl. "Stab me in the back be what she's done."

"'Tis a wound you show no signs of ill from," the older girl choked out, her nails digging crescents into his wrist.

"Aye, and she feels remorse for it. Don't you, Bede? Please, she meant no disrespect, milord, she was trying to protect me."

"Una, tell him nothing. Let the cur rot in hell for all we care."

"Keep your tongue behind those teeth." Gawain flashed his fangs at her before turning back to the youngster at his knee. "How many more are there?"

"What?"

"A man such as him would travel with two or

three more...where would they be?"

"He was alone, milord." The girl tugged again. "Please, sir, Bede meant only to save me."

Heaving a breath, Gawain dropped the girl, flashing her dagger before her eyes then sliding in into his belt. A pull on the hilt and one sickening squick and his sword was free of the human's remains. Hunger tightened in his gut, the need to feed overpowering. Sniffing at the blood, he made a face and wiped his sword clean before sliding it into his sheath. He hadn't drank rancid blood in a millennia and he wasn't about to now.

He glanced at the other humans hovering together, their fear a stomach twisting stench. Which of the lot was the one King Hemat sought? None appeared more than terrified mortal females, none except the one standing close to him. The faint hiss of a serpent's tongue in his ear.

Next to him, the babe clung to his hand. The elder girl glared at him, her breasts heaving, the tattered remains of her clothing offering little to ward off the night's chill.

It would be one of these two, but which? Instinct told him both were important.

The weight of stares upon his shoulders pulled him from his thoughts and he glanced around. They were too exposed, too vulnerable.

"By what name are you addressed?" The younger girl smiled at him.

"There's no time. Come." Grabbing her arm, Gawain glanced around, unease flitting along his skin. There were more out there, watching them. Dorstan's warning echoed in his mind. He had to get the child to safety, which meant getting to a gate on this side of his world.

"You're not taking..." Scrambling from the ground, the dark-haired girl darted over to slap at his hands. "You're not taking her. Leave her be, you...you..." Bede's voice stuttered to a halt, her eyes widening when he turned to her. "Dear gods above." She stumbled back, her hands pressed to her mouth. "No, 'tis not possible. They were only dreams...nightmares. Hardly omens..."

"She's coming with me." He leaned in, her warm, sweet breath ghosting over his flesh. "I've a task, and I'll not leave it unfinished. Not for a weak mortal who knows nothing of gratitude."

Straightening, Una's arm still within his grasp, he strode into the forest, the mist swirling around his ankles. He hid a smile at the faint echo of Bede's heart beating, the furious tattoo marking the time it took her to decide to follow him. He listened to the others scurry into the forest, the thought of how they escaped as fleeting as smoke through a keyhole. With a glance through the darkness, he turned.

Only the faltering steps of the babe halted him deep within the cover of trees. He glanced upward. The dark velvet of night was peeling away to reveal the pale blue of a daylight sky.

"We rest here. Draw a fire," he ordered, his fingers clenching his sword. "Daylight already. Was later than she said. Dangerous to be out, but no relief from it." Shaking off his displeasure, Gawain appraised the situation. He had two females in his care, one no older than those who served their queen…the other older, her curves pressing against the thin material of her wrap. The elder, Bede, her name was Bede, Gawain grumbled to himself, be of more help. If she could be convinced to do so. He turned and stared at her, a warmth creeping through his body.

Bede worked quickly, her dark hair falling over her forehead to hide her delicate features. In the muted light she looked innocent, ageless. He felt an unfamiliar draw toward her. Like an invisible thread, he could feel himself being pulled closer, his balance off kilter. Her scent rested on his tongue, sweeter than wine or blood. It flirted with his control, pushing him toward the brink.

Gawain licked his lips, his eyes tracing the pale column of her neck. His fangs sharpened, the need to bury them in the throbbing vein stronger than his conditioning…yet he held himself back. To drink of a woman was to lower himself to those of the

27

Saltar's Keir-Tak ruthless, lawless clan, and he refused to sink below his station.

With a guttural oath, he spun to pace the confines of the small clearing. There would be no travel until sundown, he couldn't risk tracing with both of them. Resigned to the wait, he settled on a log and picked up a stone. His recent feed meant that sleep would not be needed for several days. Instead, he focused on planning their journey.

* * * *

"Would it not be best to travel now, during the day rather than in the dark of night?" Bede chattered. "The sun is high and provides—"

Mortals, they understood nothing. Gawain looked upward and swore profusely. He twisted around and glared at the woman sitting a short distance away. Huddled near the small fire, her body trembled from the damp cold clinging to the air. Her thin shift offered little protection from the chill. Her blue fingers were tangled in a threadbare wrap which offered little in the way of cover. Her fingers had a sickly pallor as she released the wrap and shifted closer to the fire, her hands coming up to cup at the flames. Modesty had been forgotten in the face of warmth.

Licking his lips, he stared at the erect nipples poking at the pale fabric. What would they taste like? The sweetest of the holy wine or as tart as aged blood? Her flesh would give beneath the points of his fangs, allowing him to draw the nectar running through the blue veins that stood out in stark relief of her skin.

"Aye, the sun is high and provides warmth to those in need of it." Gawain trailed the stone down his sword. "But we wait for night to fall. It is by my order, and you'd do well to recall such things, girl." His ears picked up the heated curse she muttered under her breath. Hiding a smile, he slid his fingers down the blade, listening to the hum of metal. The blade sang to him, reminding him of its power, its purpose, as he trailed the stone over it once more.

The gatekeeper for this area would be hard to find. She was a woman prone to isolating herself, powerful, mysterious, and filled with a bitter distrust of all species. The last who had sought her out had lost a hand for their troubles. Still, he would need her gift to get the two females back.

Frustration broiled like hunger, every inch of him aching with it as he rose to pace the confines. Two females, weak, mortal, what would the king need of them? More important perhaps, what would he have to pay to get them back? Hemat had sent enough gold with him to get the one he wanted back, but there was no way to know which girl it was. Unfortunately, until Gawain was certain who it was he would need to consider paying for both of them. Perhaps he could barter with a keeper, but it was unlikely.

Licking his fangs, he moaned at the soft, sweet taste of blood upon his tongue. He stumbled, the hunger pushing against his control. Another day and he'd have to feed, a fact he knew should not be. He'd drank well, dining on the supplest of hosts before Dorstan had seen to it he'd been cast from the court. The elder had insisted Gawain would not be allowed to return until he'd regained his honor. As if Dorstan was so honorable. The man was driven by greed and lust and cared nothing for those who didn't fit into his perceptions of how things should be.

A simple task had become much more complicated. If he didn't return, the king would surely garner him a painful death at the hands of the King's current guard. To return alone would garner him nothing save the loss of what little rank he still held. Returning with the girls would earn him his position as king's guard back. Beneath the surface, however, there was something more, some thread beneath drawing his attention yet waiting in the shadows.

He knew Dorstan would have no issue with telling lies, increasing the weight of his failure tenfold. Under such trickery Hemat would blame him, punish him for his lack of intent. Aye, the king would label him a renegade. Shunned for not following the king's orders, he'd be relegated even further to the fringes of society.

"There's a farmstead east of here." Una's soft voice drew his attention to where she lay staring into the flames. Could you not hunt there?"

"How..." Gawain narrowed his eyes on her. A hard knot formed in his gut, distrust like venom in his blood. "What do you..."

"You don't feed on women and children." Una sat up, her back pressing against his knees. "It is clear to me. You've two who are worthy prey here. We are weak compared to you, but you're thinking of hunting other prey rather than drinking our blood. When your mind is not consumed with thoughts of your king and one whom you hate. Fate is a fickle creature, and what may appear in one manner may not wear the mask you see in truth."

"What nonsense you speak." Gawain scoffed, ice crawling through his veins.

"Bede sees more than she knows, knows more than she believes, but 'tis started. You've a task, yes, but to prove victorious, you need her." Una turned to him, a smile on her face. "Half a day east lays your prey, but another comes. One who will be here before the darkness rises."

"Foolish child, you talk of things you know nothing of."

Una stood, patted his cheek, and shrugged, her voice dropping to the barest hint of sound. "I speak of what I see, vampire. You can hide behind your gruffness all you want but your soul is clean. You desire something you've never had, yet fear failure. Put such thoughts from your mind, you'll be victorious and restored to position within your king's eyes."

Gawain tensed, clenching his fists at her words and gaped at her. "How do you—"

Una offered a small smile. "I am aware of much, Gawain. More than any of the mortals we will encounter. It does not take but a moment to see what drives you is vastly different than what drives them. I knew it as soon as you stepped from the shadows. Do not worry about Bede, she is lost in thought and won't hear but what she desires to. Already she plots her escape—but it is not an escape from you she yearns for. Have faith, milord. Success is within your grasp."

Stupefied, Gawain watched her walk away. Her words bounced around his mind before settling. He grinned. She had revealed herself finally. His task was uncovered. He had to get the babe back. To be so young and know so much. It was becoming clearer and clearer who they had sent him to retrieve.

Tonight he would feed and scry for the gatekeeper. Once located, he'd take the youngster and return to his king. With the babe in hand, his failures would be forgiven and he would rise to his place among his brethren.

It would be necessary to leave the elder girl. She would only slow him down, and the king had said nothing of bringing her back. Gawain focused on her trembling frame, his heart sinking. She had no place among his kind - they would feed on her until she was no more and then toss her aside. He forced the niggling emotion away. Soon he'd be alone, sipping on whiskey, safe within the confines of his cabin as he wanted.

Chapter Three

Gawain paced through the shadows along the edge of their small camp. His skin crawling, he cast a glance around him. There was danger. Every instinct honed by years on the battlefield screamed it. Beneath the hard binding of his ribs, his heart thundered, echoing the soft throb of Bede's in the stillness. A half smile curved her lips upward, her head bent close to her sister's. Bede ran her fingers through Una's long hair, smoothing the tangles out with care.

The song she was humming so softly was familiar—achingly so, yet he could not place it. Perhaps it was one his own mother had sung for him when he was but a child. He inhaled, a ghostly image skittering through his mind of a dark-haired woman with pale eyes and a tender smile.

He moved closer, an invisible hand guiding him toward the pair. Silent, standing behind her, he closed his eyes, the soothing sound of his mother's voice playing in his memory. Her voice stroked over him, soothing his mind, easing his heart as he let the words, the melody, slip past his defenses.

Every instinct in his body screamed at him to get closer. Drink. Drink. Sate the hunger. She is mortal, weak. Little more than food. Drink and see the hunger satisfied.

Gawain growled and slammed his fist into the tree beside him. No. He would not. Drinking from a woman was beyond bad luck, it was downright foolish. Aye, he shook his head, everyone was aware a woman's blood was sweeter, but to be truly satisfied, one had to drink more frequently than with a man.

Frail as women were, the likelihood of killing was higher.

Unless the one you drank from was your mate.

Then it was a rarity one would kill...but it happened. There was only one instance he knew of, and had no desire to follow in the path of one who was beyond death. A shudder shook his frame and he spat. Sunwalkers were reviled, hideous creatures. Driven by an unquenchable hunger. So desperate to drink, unable to do so. Hungering for their lost mate. Their lack of control ultimately cost their loved one a life.

Gawain raked a hand through his hair, contrary to most of his brethren, he had never felt a deep compunction to be mated. A female was a bothersome chore. She would be in the way, constantly nagging, interfering with his work. A soft body to warm his bed, to give him children, to know the pleasures of which he had long denied himself, a tiny voice whispered. One to ease the loneliness, to ease the burden of his exile.

Shaking off his thoughts, he turned away. He needed to separate the sisters. First, though, he needed to feed. Mayhap he should seek the farmstead. In this time, vampires were only stories told to scare children. No one would even question him.

He ducked beneath a branch and stepped deeper into the shadows of the woods. Earthy, the soft scent carried on the wind stirred his urge to hunt. Faint but easily identifiable, the tang of a young man's pulsing blood drifted through the leaves. A slow smirk crossed Gawain's face. A few hours and his prey would be within striking distance.

"Tonight." Gawain nodded. "Tonight I'll hunt, then return to the king."

* * * *

Bede watched the tall, stalwart man prowling the edge of camp, sitting up a little straighter when he stepped around a patch of sunlight without breaking stride. Thigh-high leather boots blended into the black pants he wore, his dark tunic covered by a long, hoodless cloak. One side of the cloak was tucked back, revealing the curve of one hip and flank. He clutched at his sword, a dark snarl twisting his features. The broadsword was far different from anything she'd seen. It was long, wide, and as straight as an arrow. Fine lines, much like the ivy that clung to the walls of the cottage, decorated it.

It was obviously the weapon of a wealthy man, a man of title, of nobility. What could such a man want with her and Una? They were paupers, lower than low. Even the Roman troops who had passed earlier in the spring had barely given them a look. She shifted, unease creeping over her. Was he a slaver? Maybe he was sent to steal them for another master. If so, he'd not find any ease in delivering them, she vowed.

"Take care, Bede." Una's soft voice drew her attention. "You've no idea what you'll find beneath the surface."

"What do you mean?"

"There is darkness there, yet it does not reach his soul. Unlike the monster who bought us, Gawain holds no desire for wealth. He does not intend to gain gold coins for the use of ourselves. Bear in mind, sister, dangerous as he may be, he will surprise you." Una met her stare. "Before this night is through, we shall need him, and his sword."

"You talk in such riddles. There is no more to him than any other man. Cold and merciless, they take and take until there is naught left. Look at Momma, she was a good woman brought down by a man."

"You confuse our savior with the men we have seen."

"I do not confuse him with anything. You are too young to recall the misery brought to Momma when Pappa took ill. Forced to live with that bastard, who sold us as Pappa wilted and died. He was a brute, selfish, cruel. A man not worthy of even a moment's notice. Gawain is no different."

"You are bitter, Bede. Gawain is nothing like those who surround us." Una shrugged, her lips lifting slightly. "What he takes shall be paid back tenfold, sister. Mark my words, you will thank him before the sun rises again. Just as you will thank him when this journey has finished and you embrace what you deny at this moment."

Bede watched her sister rise and begin to pace behind the strange man who spared her naught a glance. Hands locked behind her back, Una stepped quickly, a studious expression on her delicate face as she shadowed him. Gawain barely looked at her. Indeed, he seemed lost in thought, in some mystery within his soul.

Turning her attention back to the fire, Bede rubbed her arms. A chill crept over her, dancing along her skin like a caress. Freedom would come, she was certain. She'd simply have to be cunning in her plotting. When next he fell to slumber, as he had to, they'd been awake for some time—he the longest of all, she would make her move. While he slept, she'd retrieve her dagger and steal away with Una. North toward the Pict territory would garner their safety, south would lead into Roman bonds. Within the ancestral peoples of her mother she would find solace and safety.

Glancing across the sun splattered clearing, she sighed. He stood, broad shoulders beneath the black leather of his cloak braced against any threat. Muscled thighs flowed down into high boots stitched with an unfamiliar design which reflected the light. He shifted, his hands coming to rest behind his back as he stared into the thick foliage.

A strange fog swirled at the edges of her vision and she blinked. Gods above what...between one blink and the next, Bede found herself washed in sensations. The forest faded into the softness of a bed, candles flickering in the darkness.

Heat suffused her flesh, wrapping tendrils along her body. Like ghostly fingers it played over her breasts, teasing her nipples. Flames flickered and danced, casting a pale, warm glow over her naked flesh.

Calloused fingertips explored hidden curves, the slight abrasions rasping over sensitive flesh.

Bolts of lightning coursed through at the sharp drag of a fang against her tender skin. The rough sweep of his tongue over an aching nipple drew a strangled moan. Her body undulated under him, hands clutching at the back of his head. She moaned with each wave of pleasure coursing through her body.

He suckled at her breast, his tongue licking along her hard nipple. Shards of molten heat shot to her throbbing folds.

Throbbing, her body writhed beneath her lover in the throes of a most pleasant ache. Her hands scrambled for purchase against hard, sweaty flesh. Muscles bunched and rolled beneath her fingers, his erect nipples teased her. His hot shaft pressed against her abdomen, rocking against her flesh with searing intent.

"Grasp my cock." His voice raked over exposed nerves as he pulled a trembling hand down to wrap around the pulsing thickness. She gasped as her fingers pressed around it but didn't meet. Her hand eased down and up, caressing gently. Molten, hard, it throbbed beneath her touch. Shy, she petted his sex, her fingers scrambling to wrap around his shaft with each thrust of his hips.

His tongue dipped into her mouth, dueling with hers, mimicking the motion of his hips. Her breath came in unsteady gasps as he teased and retreated, drawing her into the dance. He suckled her tongue, his fingers sliding down her body, trailing like brands between her breasts to slide through the moist curls at the apex of her thighs.

"Please, gods. Oh, please." She whimpered, all inhibitions gone in the rising storm of desire. Her body lurched when his nails scored the hood of her sensitive clit. Daggers of sensation ripped through her, the walls of her core clenching, pulsing with the need to have his hard cock buried within its walls.

Hunger like none she'd ever felt wrapped around her swollen sex. She raised her hips in silent supplication. Screams of pleasure escaped her throat, and she arched into his touch as he slid a thick finger into her body. Tilting her head back, she lifted off the rough woolen pallet, her grasp tightening around his hard shaft. Each slow glide of his digit teased, fed the fire until she longed for the flames.

"Tighter, leannan, tighter. I want to feel you clasp me…to milk my cock." He grabbed her hand, forcing her to tighten her hold on him. "The head, gods, leannan, rub the head. Taste me."

She moaned softly at the slick stickiness oozing from the slit along the head of his shaft. Her mouth watered as each glide of her thumb brought forth more liquid. Desperate to taste him, to bath in his essence, she tugged on her hand.

"Nooo." She tossed her head as he pulled his finger from her sex. Arching her hips, she rolled them, shamelessly begging for him to sink back into her depths. "Please."

"Nay, I need to taste you." He licked his finger, his tongue swirling around the glistening digit. A look of utter lust twisted his face. She watched, fascinated as he lapped at her essence, sucking it off his finger like honey.

Her tongue glided along her bottom lip. Holding his stare, she raised her hand, licking the moisture from her thumb. A mixture of sweet and salty, she moaned at the heady taste and sensation. Would his cock taste as delicious? Wiggling, she began to turn only to have him halt her with a rough hand on her hip.

"More, I want…"

"Oh, Bede, I'll give it all to you," he grunted. His fingers tangled in her hair, he lifted her toward him. "I'll let you take me in your mouth, to run your tongue along the head. To suck the very milk from me." She whimpered with each statement. "But first, I want to drink of you. To taste your honey and have you scream my name."

"I want your…"

"Lie back then." He shifted, pressing her back into the pallet. He turned, his thick legs on either side of her head. "Open for me, my leannan, open for me."

She moaned as he pressed hot, open-mouthed kisses to her stomach. Reaching up, she grasped his weeping shaft and guided it to her lips. Her tongue darted out to lick along the head. Dipping into the thin slit, tasting the sweet nectar there. Lips parted, she swirled her tongue along the crown before guiding him in…

"Bede, help me!" Una's scream yanked her from the mist and into the moment.

Her body thrummed with energy, a weight to her limbs as she stumbled to her feet. Bede shook her head and whirled around her. Her stomach dropped to her feet.

Gods, no. Men in the familiar red of the Roman army poured into camp. Swords clashing, screams of rage filled the air. A guttural roar shook the ground beneath her feet and Bede twisted on her feet.

Surrounded by three soldiers, Gawain held them at bay with ease. The air around him shimmered and crackled with energy. Muscles clenched and flexed with each swing of his blade. A smirk twisted his face. He toyed with them. The realization stuck like a fist and she focused on her sister.

Una stood an arms length away, frozen with

terror as two Roman soldiers approached, their swords raised. Screaming, she snatched Una from the path of a soldier, his sword whistling through the air again and again as he was determined to kill. Desperate, her mind racing, Bede searched the forest, there had to be an escape. Somewhere safe to go. A branch cracked and she glanced upward. The trees. Of course. Tightening her grip, she leaned closer to her sister. "Go, to the trees, Una. Quickly now."

Una sobbed, her hands clutching at Bede. "What of you?"

"It matters little. Go. Now, Una." Steel ran through her tone as she shoved her sister toward the nearest tree. Three soldiers closed in, their swords dangling limply from their fingers as they appraised her. Lust flickered as they took in the threadbare shift, the rise and fall of her breasts. Bede swallowed, retreating. There were too many of them to escape. She backed up, one slow, measured step at a time. As if guided by an invisible hand a thick branch appeared next to her foot and she lunged for it.

Heavy and thick the gnarled wood bit into her palms. Bede swallowed and gripped the makeshift club tighter. The pain of her fear faded slightly, and she jabbed at one eager soldier who darted forward. Agony filled his scream as the wood cut through tender flesh, drawing blood. Swinging it wildly, she prayed they'd leave her, but held little hope they would answer. Her prayer was wasted on fickle gods who ignored the mortals they watched over.

Hard arms wrapped around her from behind her, the hot wash of stale breath against her neck making her skin crawl. Choking back a scream, she struggled, kicking and biting as they ripped at her clothes. As she twisted and struggled, her nails scored the face of one, drawing blood. The screams and laughter of the men rose with her screams as she fought desperately, their hands pawing at her body.

The rancid stench of their sweaty, filthy bodies filled her nostrils. Gagging and choking as one tightened his grip around her throat, she fought on, darkness closing in. Kicking at her attackers, she grunted when her foot connected with the soft flesh of one's groin.

As quickly as the assault started, it ended. Gasping, tears racing down her face, she glanced up. A sword quivered from Gawain's chest as he hovered over her, his face twisted into a dark mask of hatred. She flinched when he pulled it free, tossing it aside. The sword shook when it landed, buried to the hilt in a nearby tree.

He lashed out, his claws slashing through flesh. Scarlett splattered on his face, his clothes, and Bede's bare flesh. A Roman soldier dangled from one hand, his chest gaping open. Blood flowed down his body to drip onto the leaves beneath him. A rattling gurgle from his lips drew a shudder as Gawain tossed him aside. He focused on the soldier climbing to his feet.

"Don't know why you're not dead, but it doesn't matter. The wench is—"

"Mine," Gawain ground out, his lips curling upward. "I do not share."

Bede's eyes widened. His fangs, long and sharp, dripped with blood. She scrambled back when he moved, grabbing the soldier and twisting him, his fingers tangling in the grubby man's hair.

"She and the babe belong to me." Guttural, his voice grated already exposed nerves before he sunk his teeth into the man's neck.

Scrambling to her feet, Bede whirled, stumbling over the broken remains of a soldier. Bile rose like a tide in her throat, bitter and acrid, as blood streamed from the soldier's throat, soaking his uniform.

"No!" Bede darted for the trees, her breath exploding on a sob. *Escape. Run.*

Branches cracked beneath her feet, each sound like thunder. Her feet slipped, sending her stumbling forward. Sobbing, Bede threw her hands out, her knees hitting the ground with a tooth jarring force. Her lungs burning, she scrambled forward, driven by an unseen whip. She had to escape.

A warm hand wrapped around her waist, pulling her back against a hard body. Gentle hands pulled her torn clothes together before they wrapped a soft cloak around her shoulders and fastened with a pin.

"Come. The moon rises." Gawain's soft voice shattered the tenuous grasp she had on control of her emotions. As if a dam had broken, they poured forth in an endless wave of sound and heat.

Screaming, her hands over her ears, she curled into a ball on the ground. Tears choked her, and her throat burned as she rocked on her haunches. Her fingers tangled in her hair, a pain unlike anything she'd felt skewering her.

Chapter Four

"Gawain?" Una's weak voice drifted from above and he looked up. The child clung to a sturdy branch, arms and legs wrapped around the trunk. Tears created pale streams down her face, the haunting look in her eyes twisted a dagger in Gawain's chest.

Was brutality and terror the way all mortals treated their females and young? The odor of the men's lust still clung to his nostrils. Putrid and grotesque, a low rumbling growl escaped him and he glanced over his shoulder. He should have shown them less kindness, they deserved a more painful death than he had delivered.

"Come, Una, we have no time to waste. We will be gone from this place before more of their ilk comes." Gawain tucked a corner of his cloak tighter around Bede's shoulders before he swept her into his arms and against his chest.

Una nodded and shimmied down the trunk to land on her feet a few steps away. Wide eyed she stared at Bede for a moment, fresh tears spilling down her face. She raised her gaze and met his stare. One brow rose and she blinked before she bent down, shoving aside the body of a soldier. With a grunt, Una tugged the tattered remains of the dead soldier's cloak around her shoulders and fell into step behind him.

"She is not weak." Una's soft voice held a note of awareness. It grated across Gawain's raw nerve and he glanced back at the child.

"Nay, she is not." Gawain adjusted Bede in his arms. "This world is beyond redemption. Females and children are not meant to be treated so harshly."

"Perhaps." Una fell silent, the crunching of the debris on the forest floor teasing his ears.

Bede's breath hitched, a harsh wracking sob shaking her body in his arms. Gawain ducked Bede's weak, flailing arm, the sound of her terror clawing at his soul. Cradling her against his chest, he stalked through the shadows. Relief filled him at the sight of several horses tethered. They needed to move, and the horses would help with their haste. The rapid patter of small feet trailed behind him.

He glanced at the back of their little entourage. The scent of the soldiers' blood soaked the air, with the sounds of their dying echoing in the night. A whisper of the gurgling and whistling of air through fading lungs teased his ears. The garbled sounds of men choking on their own blood stained the silence.

They would have provided a bounty of blood for

him - but the thought of the mortal's blood within his belly was enough to turn it. Nay, they were fit only for the carrion eaters of this realm.

A tempest of heat and blood-lust lashed at him with each broken sob from the woman in his arms. Her physical wounds would heal rapidly. Those unseen, he was certain would not easily heal. His fangs lengthened, sharpening with each step, and he tightened his grip. Stopping next to the horses, he frowned, every instinct telling him to delay their ending.

"She's terrified." Una clung to Bede's hand. "Those men were going to..."

"Think not of such matters." Gawain set Bede atop a horse and turned to grab Una. With an agile swing he set her behind Bede. "Hang on, child. To the north there is shelter for you both. There is one there who would serve my kind. Safety lies that way and that is where you will go."

"What of you?" Una grabbed his arm, fear tightening her frail voice. "Are you..."

"Nay, I'll not leave you. I can make good speed. There's discord on the wind, I can sense it." Gawain felt his unease flare, a shiver racing down his spine at the distant, vacant look that settled on Una's face.

"He comes." Una focused up the trail, her brows

drawn together. "Not mortal, but not immortal either. A man cursed with an empty soul. Gawain, the one ahead of us is far more dangerous than the Romans."

Gawain bit back a growl. Of course the enemy would send someone to ensure his success. Dorstan had no faith in his loyalty. "Do not worry about him child, we will make haste and be away from here before he finds us."

Swinging onto the back of the nearest horse, he gathered both reins and turned northward. Kicking the horses into a gallop, he wondered if he could possibly outrun the trouble that was coming.

"He seeks something, someone," she called. "I don't believe him to be human, vampire. He is something else. A twisted soul longing for an end but trapped by the will of another. He will not turn back."

His heart stuttered, Gods be merciful. The one who stalked them now was beyond redemption. Nay, it was not Dorstan then. No, another, far worse than anything Hemat could send against him. It was a sad day when she sent a sunwalker to hunt a human. Gawain shrugged, hoping the child wouldn't pick up on his unease. They could not linger. If Angor walked the mortal realm it was only a matter of time before they met - and he would not risk the child, or Bede's safety. "Matters not, young one. Hold on, we've distance to cover."

Whipping both horses into a full run, Gawain cut off the road, through the underbrush. There was too much risk on the road, soldiers, bandits, slave traders... men with no honor would do anything to seize the bounty he had. Neither Una nor Bede would be a pawn in their greed. Off the trail, there would be safety from the mortals.

If it was as Una had said and someone had sent a Sunwalker after them he would need to put distance between them and the carnage. If it was who he thought it to be, time was not on their side. Damn the gods for their fickle nature.

He sucked in a deep breath, the fading scent of terror fading beneath the bitter tang of blood. Decay hung heavy in the night air, a solid odor he recognized. One that turned his stomach and he whipped his mount faster. With the moon rising, he'd be able to travel freely. By dawn they'd be nearer the cottage of one who could help.

* * * *

Bede jerked upright, her body tense at the squeal of horses and the thunder of hooves. She gasped, a scream dying in her throat at the strange, pale figure standing in the roadway. The moon cast a silver light over the stranger making him even eerier. Was it a demon risen to destroy all in his path? Or was it something far worse?

"What..."

"Hush." Gawain's harsh tone was like a slap in the face. In an instant, fury roared forward to crowd her control.

She leaned forward sucking in a breath.

"Be still, Bede." Una's soft tone eased her anger. "He comes."

"Who?"

Una nodded past Gawain. "There's a darkness, a death about him reaching into his soul, yet he keeps it chained. Mind him, Bede, Gawain will not lead you wrong."

"Be still. I would see you both safe away from here. If he thinks he can sway you he will do so." Gawain raised a hand, his claws flared. "The one who controls him has no heart, only a lust for gold and blood. He is unworthy to be in either of your presences."

"Give me the young one." Like sludge, the stranger's voice seeped through the darkness. "That is all I seek."

"No," Bede cried, clutching Una to her. "Gawain, milord…"

"Give her to me and you shall pass. Don't make this more arduous than it needs be." The stranger withdrew his sword, the pale light catching on the curved blade.

"I'll take your head before I surrender either of them." Gawain drew his sword, the moonlight dancing along the edge of the blade.

"Why must you challenge me on this?" Soundlessly, he disappeared, reappearing mere feet from the horses. "You do not understand, Gawain, there are things that must come to pass before the end. I have been commanded to bring the child to my mistress. You of all of our kind should understand what it means to face failure in an order. Take heed, Gawain, give me the girl and see yourself and the woman free of me this night."

"Anagor, you are an even bigger fool than I dared imagine." Gawain dismounted, his attention never wavering from the intruder. "It will garner you no favors, only certain death."

His rough chuckle filled the air, a desperate keening sound that sent chills racing down Bede's spine. "Death would serve me well, my lord. Sadly, through a bitter twist of fate, death has been forsaken to me. Give me the young one and I shall depart from your path."

"Heed me, Anagor, I will not turn her over to the likes of you. She is under my protection, my banner. If you do not turn from this madness it will be your heart upon my blade."

"Do not tempt me, Gawain. Do as I ask and you can keep the harlot." Anagor scratched along the thing column of his throat. "I've no desire to be here any longer than necessary. Yield the field to me for the moment."

Bede gasped, her spine straightening at the sneer in his voice. "How dare…"

"Hush, Bede," Una whispered, her fingers tightening painfully around her hand. "Let Gawain handle him."

"I'm tiring of having to—"

"There are things in motion, sister," Una's voice lowered, and she pressed closer. "Pride will get you nowhere save a grave. You must put your faith in him. He risks life and limb to keep us safe."

The heavy throbbing of metal clashing split the night. Gaping in horror, she winced when the stranger's sword cut through the clasp of Gawain's tunic, sending the fabric pooling around his feet.

Gawain swirled in a dark cloud, appearing behind their assailant, his sword shearing off locks of pale hair. His eyes darkened, glowing with inner fury. He barely spared her a glance as he struck again and again, his sword clashing with Anagor's. Blow after blow, grunts and words in a foreign tongue spewed forth.

The horses started, nickering in alarm when the blades connected under the force of a heavy blow sending them flying. It would have almost been comical to see the hilts waving in the air if the two men wrestling before her held nothing back. Her heart stuttered in her chest, they fought to the death, she was certain.

Agonized screams shattered the silence as they fought, blood splattering on the leaves beneath their feet.

Gawain reared back. Long, bloody gouges ran across his face. His lip split to the bone as he swung hard, sending the stranger flying into a tree. His back had no more than hit the trunk, sending it careening to the ground, before he was flying at Gawain, fangs dripping, nails gleaming in the moonlight.

"Gods above, we have to help him." Bede turned to her sister, her body already leaning, preparing to dismount.

Her heart raced, her attention focused on Gawain. His massive frame absorbed the blows from his enemy. Round after round fell, pushing him back, before he struck out. With each passing heartbeat, his stance changed, becoming harder, more predatory, blood frothing at his lips.

She cringed with each thud of bone meeting flesh. The grunts of pain were swallowed by the growls of rage. Blood splattered the leaves, glittering in the light of the moon. Masculine voices spewed forth their rage, their disgust, in a language she didn't understand, yet the violence of their hatred flowed like water.

"You cannot help him." Una's dead tone sent a shard of fear up Bede's spine.

"Why not?" Bede whirled to stare at her sister, her jaw slack.

"You are not meant to." Una met her eyes. "This stops here, now. We both know it. You have but to listen to your heart to know this. My place is not here, it never was." Tears gathered on her pale lashes, and a small, sad smile tugged at her lips.

"Una, you speak in such riddles and nonsense. Of course your place…" Bede froze at the eerie snarl which erupted from before the horses. Gawain lay on the hard ground, his chest split wide open, blood streaming down his sides. The flash of his white skin stark in the darkness. Legs braced, his sword in his hands, the stranger stared at her for a moment before burying the heavy blade into Gawain's body.

"No!" Bede screamed, all but falling from the horse, the need to get to Gawain stronger than her fear. Stronger than her concern even for her sister who picked up Gawain's wrap, draped it over her shoulders, and stepped closer. Scrambling across the ground, Bede tripped, crawling the last few feet separating them. Her knees felt each prickle of stone, each scratch of a twig, but she ignored the discomfort.

"You wretch! Look what you've done," Bede sobbed, holding Gawain's head. Her throat burned, the scalding of tears on her face colder than ice in winter. Bede's hand shot out to grab Una as she stepped past her. "You won't take her—"

"Bede." Una knelt, her young eyes filled with wisdom far beyond her summers. "This must be. You'll not be alone and you're safe. Darkness can only claim what it has already weakened. His soul is untouched—and needs yours. Bede, I see your future, see your world. It has always been coming to this point. To this moment. If you do not let me go, everything you care about - everything that is meant to be yours crumbles. You give to him something more than any other, something he needs. You need it as well, my sister. I can see the power flowing between you, the warmth which will keep you safe." Una pressed a quick kiss to her cheek and rose to step over Gawain's still body. "I'm ready."

"No!" Bede's agonized scream echoed in the night's stillness as Una and the stranger vanished into thin air, leaving her alone with a battered and broken warrior. Beneath her knees the hot pool of his blood soaked into her clothing and the ground.

Bowing her head, Bede sobbed uncontrollably.

Chapter Five

Una was gone.

Gawain lay near death, felled by the very man who had stolen her sister. Bede swiped at the tears on her cheeks. What fate did the gods have in store for her? When would the nightmare be over and she could rest? Nay she would find her sister and any who stood—

"Tell me, why do you weep?" Faint, a note of warmth curled through the whisper clinging to the edge of her awareness.

Bede jerked upright and scanned the darkness. Thin beams of silver cascaded through the canopy, dancing across the ground. A branch cracked and the rustle of leaves hinted at movement. A woman stepped from between two thick trees, her flowing gown caressing the forest floor. Dark hair done in an elaborate coil peeked from beneath the gossamer thin veil covering her head. The moonlight glinted off the jewels around her throat and wrists.

A woman of breeding, of social standing. She paced across the ground, her hands clasped at her waist.

"Who are you?" Bede demanded, her fingers knotting in Gawain's tunic.

"Do you truly not know?"

Her gut twisting, Bede inched her hand across Gawain's chest. Maybe if she could get to his sword. "Just another Roman's whore. There is nothing to steal. No slave to punish."

"Roman? You think me to be human." The woman chuckled, a musical sound that filled the air around them. "I have not been mortal for lifetimes, child."

"Stay away."

"Or you'll what? Drink me to death? 'Tis been tried before, Bede of the Woods, by beings far more powerful than you. Indeed, it is what brought me to this point."

The elaborate hilt of Gawain's dagger slid into view and Bede swallowed. Finally, favor from the gods. She reached for the dagger, her fingers closing around the leather and steel. "What do you want? We've no coin for you to take. I've nothing save what you see." Bede kept the woman in her line of sight, her stomach a hard painful knot.

"I care not for your gold or silver, Bede. Oh no, it is not why I have come." The woman stepped closer still, the toes of her sandals brushing against Gawain's leg. "It has been an age since I felt such agony pierce through me. The loss of a child, a lover-to-be, a life. Reason rough, I think for anyone to know pain."

"Then I suggest you go find the cause of your pain, my lady, and leave us be." Bede pointed the dagger at the other woman. "Else I shall send you from this life and to the next."

"Tsk, tsk, child. I believe this would be better." The woman grasped the sword hilt and pulled it from Gawain's body.

"No." Bede lurched forward, her hand outstretched as she grabbed for the sword. The warm, bloody metal slicing through the flesh of her hand. Biting back a cry, she gripped the blade tighter. "You would kill him without a thought."

Gaway groaned in response, his fingers already twitching. The woman shifted and nodded toward Gawain's prone body. "He'll wake soon. Ravenous, the need to feed strong after losing so much blood."

"He won't harm me." Confidence, certainty boiled within her at the very notion. No, Gawain would do her no harm. "You, on the other hand..."

Heaving a breath, the woman smiled and knelt beside her. "Come, Bede, truly you do not know the full meaning of what this night has come to? Shall I explain?"

Bede gnashed her teeth together at the stranger's haughty air.

"Ah it appears I must. Fear not for Una. She is safe, and she will make her way back to you in time. You were never meant to follow the same path, child. Your fate is different than hers. Your place, somewhere far from where Una must go. For now, you must learn to rely on Gawain. He is a warrior without equal, a man prepared to die for you."

"One who even now bleeds out on the floor of this wretched place. Aided by your wilful ripping out of the blade."

"He is the last of the chosen, the last of my most sacred orders. Gawain is everything a man could be, and so much more than some will ever understand. He is one who, if you trust within both his and your own heart, will return to you something stolen from you long, long ago."

Her eyes narrowed when the strange woman ran her fingers through his hair. Slapping her hand away, Bede tugged him closer, his chest rising slowly beneath her.

"Don't touch—"

"I have no interest in your little vampire. I have more important matters to attend to." She brushed an invisible bit of dust off her robe. "Saltar even now is stirring, his bonds weakened by the meddling of another with her own purpose. There is a war brewing, one that will have far reaching consequences. It will spill from our world into this one, from immortal to mortal."

"So you say. You have not even given your name, not that I believed you would. Your threats of war fall on deaf ears. Saltar or whatever you call him has no power over me."

"Ah, Bede. A true daughter of fire and blood. You are your mother's daughter, Bede. Take heed, Bede, it is within the arms of the man before you that you will find the answers. He will give to you that which was stolen. It is time, time for my followers to return to their roots. For those who are pure of heart to rise above Saltar's treachery and rejoin their kind. I pray you understand, Bede, these are dangerous times. I will be watching."

Turning, the woman strode into the trees and vanished.

"I promise you, no harm shall befall young Una. She is of my blood, same as you, and will be safe." The soft promise danced through Bede's mind, leaving her with a hollow feeling in her chest and a fresh wave of tears coursing down her face.

Exhaustion settled like a heavy weight about her, pulling her deeper and deeper into darkness.

* * * *

The echo of battle drifted on the warm wind soaking through the thin walls of the tent Bede stood in. Her long, sheer skirt fluttered like wings around her legs. Pushing the curtain back, she stared at the expanse of ground before her with a practical eye. Men and beasts cluttered the battlefield. The smell of blood hung heavy in the air. Moans of agony mingled with the clash of steel.

Her eyes focused on one warrior, his massive chest glistening in the moonlight. His sword slid into the scabbard, his attention on his men as they gathered. She knew they'd feed on those wounded, those whose hearts still beat with a steady if weak pulse.

"Impressive, isn't he?" Behind her, a lone woman lounged on the dais, her pale skin flickering gold in the light of the flames from the torches.

"Do you have nothing to do but disturb the victors?"

"Nay, I wish to keep track of my warriors. He's well earned his reward."

"I think you need to concern yourself with those who are more inclined—"

"Come, Bede, you fool yourself if you think that I would want to concern myself with anything beyond the delight of having one so valiant on the field of battle rewarded with a beautiful mate. Bid me reward him and I shall give you him. A daughter of the Ker-etsa is deserving of such a man."

"Be gone, goddess. You bother me." She turned away, her attention focusing on the man striding from the field. 'Twas true, he deserved one worthy of him. Her fangs sharpened, ached to sink into his glistening flesh.

"It is as you desire," Amuliana whispered into her ear a moment before she vanished.

Bede swallowed, her body on fire as he tossed aside his sword, his glowing eyes locked on hers. Heat pooled, settling between her legs in a sudden flood. Heavy throbbing in her breasts echoed in the pulsing blood beneath flesh.

"A woman worthy," he growled, grabbing her hair to pull her against his body. His fingers dug into the flesh of her ass as he ground his growing erection against her. "I could smell the sweet scent of your blood in battle, taste the nectar between your lips on my tongue. You were made for me."

"As you were for me," she purred. "Warrior, prince, servant to our queen. Are you hot for me? Want me with the same need I feel for you?" Tracing her lips with her tongue, she toyed with his nipple, her nails dragging over hard muscles. Her nostrils flared at the scent of sex and blood, the urge to devour, to stalk and claim powerful. Dipping her head, she licked along his collarbone, her sharp teeth scratching at his flesh.

"Indeed," he said, jerking her head back. She screamed in pleasure as he sank his fangs into her neck. The sensation of suckling at her throat reached deep into her core, and waves of pleasure spread throughout her body. It settled into a rhythmic pounding between her legs, her clit pulsing with each draw on her neck.

She arched against him, flames licking at the hard press of his erection against her stomach. Pulling back, she licked her lips before rising to her toes, her tongue tracing over his lips, lapping at the blood there. A moan of desire escaped as he opened his mouth, his tongue darting out to tangle with hers. Sweet, the succulent taste of blood hung rich and thick on her tongue.

Voracious, his tongue swept into her mouth. Dueling with hers, low growls from both lovers vibrated through her breasts, reaching deep into her soul to stoke the fires of lust. His fingers bit into her ass, and he lifted her slightly, wrapping her legs around his waist as he thrust against her hot, wet core.

"Hot, tight," he groaned, his lips pressed against her throat. "Sweeter than honey, aren't you?"

"Milord." She dropped her head back, her hair brushing the ground. "You're merciless, 'tis cruel to tease me thus."

"You've yet to see anything." He strode through the tent flaps to drop her atop his bed, his weight pressing her deeper into the furs.

* * * *

Scorching pain lanced through Gawain's chest, ripping him from the darkest depths of his own mind. A harsh tremble raced through his body and he sucked in a breath. Embers flared to life in his blood, coursing through his body. His skin prickled with electricity, his cock stirring to life. He groaned at the sudden hardening between his legs.

Inhaling, he twisted his head, his gaze landing on Bede's curled body next to him. Warm, soft curves pressed against him, tears dried on her pale cheeks. Her hands clenched around his shoulders. Yet he sensed no pain, no injury. Rather, the rising scent of her essence tickled his senses, teased his nostrils. He reached down, palming his shaft. It jumped beneath his touch.

Eight hundred and twenty years he'd longed for, dreamed of a mate—even as he pushed his need, his longing aside. Now, he faced a mate before him, ripe, sweet. There was nothing stopping him from taking her.

"Bloody hell," he ground out, rolling away, his eyes narrowing dangerously. His gums ached, the flesh parting as his fangs slid down. They dripped with hunger. He hovered over her, his gaze fixed on the pulse at the base of her throat. "No, it will not be me." With a furious roar he turned away, his body wracked with need, aching.

"Wha… Milord?" Bede's soft whisper stroked along his shaft, yanking at the boundaries of his control.

Without a word, he inhaled, his fists clenched at his side. He teleported—it was best to feed one hunger when he couldn't feed the other.

Chapter Six

Bede tugged the leather cloak around her shoulders and inhaled the rich scent of wood smoke, wine, and something earthier. It stirred something within her soul, banking the embers of a fire she feared. Nay, she would not allow herself to dwell on want or need. Lust was a tool to men and would serve her naught.

The night air pressed in on her like a warm embrace. A gust of wind stirred the hair at her temple and she glanced up. Gawain stood before her, legs braced. The stain of blood along his tunic in stark contrast to the pale fabric.

Gawain licked his lips, the tip of one tooth flashing. The knot in her belly, she hadn't realized, was there, loosened. He had come back. Alone, but he had returned.

"You should have kept moving, Bede." Gawain reached out, pulling her to her feet. He cast a look over her, from the top of her head to her feet. A subtle nod and he turned away.

"Did you find where my sister has been taken?" Bede cursed the faint tremor in her voice. Damn the weakness. She would not break - not until the man who had stolen Una paid with his life.

"I didn't seek her out." Gawain inhaled. "Her fate is no longer within my hands. She is safe, for the moment."

Biting back a sharp retort, Bede stomped up to him. "She is a child. That...that monster stole her and you would not leave her to his demented mercy?"

"Angor will never harm her. He is beyond any lust - be it for blood or wet–" Gawain swallowed. "There are other, more pressing concerns we must face. One of which is to move."

"And if I refuse to go anywhere without my sister?"

Gawain chuckled, a dark sound filled with smoke and embers. He smiled, his lips pulled back to reveal his still pinkish colored fangs. A zing ripped through her, drawing a shuddery breath. Good Gods, she couldn't take note - no, no, she would not.

Gawain stepped into her space, a hint of the metallic odor of blood on his hot breath. "Angor is not the only monster stalking the night, woman. Stay, if you are of a mind to deal with the lusts of men."

Bede choked back a gasp and whirled, scanning the shadows. Had the soldiers followed? Or were there others out there waiting for her to drop her guard? "You lie."

"No. I do not. Pick the beast you would rather deal with, woman. I've no time for indecision."

"You will help me find my sister."

"No, I will not."

Ice crawled through her veins. Surely he wouldn't turn from the safety of a child? Una had sacrificed so Gawain...he owed her. "Why not? I'll not leave my defenseless sister to the mercy of some monster because you're off doing..." Rage spewed like lava as she gaped at him.

"Anagor will not harm her," he ground out, the muscle in his jaw jumping.

"How can you be so certain? Did you even try..." Bede gasped, his hand suddenly tightening around her neck. Desperate, she reached up, clinging to his wrists. A tiny voice whispered in her ear, the soft words erasing any fear she felt. Gawain would do nothing to harm her. She stared into his darkened gaze, the anger, the hunger, the lust bare for her to see.

Shuddering, she could feel the heat build in her body. Was this how it felt when Una had her visions? Did she feel as though she were watching a scene rather than being in it? Such a possibility was impossible, Bede gulped, she did not have the gift of sight. There was no way this was one—they were standing in a cool, damp forest, his clothes shredded by a blade, his chest bare beneath, dried blood streaking the pale flesh.

"Woman, you'd try the patience of an angel, and I am hardly one. It is impossible to track a trace, especially when he is cursed with the ability to walk in the sun. Now, I will find the babe. To do so means I must find one with the gift of sight. Keep your tongue behind your teeth and do not—"

"I will not rest until my sister is safe." Bede smacked his arm. "Not even the likes of you will keep me from seeking—"

"Gods above, you foolish girl. She will be safe with Anagor. He does not feed, he doesn't breed, and in fact he is walking dead." Gawain's hot breath whispered over her flesh. She swallowed when he leaned closer to her. "'Tis you in more danger than she. You would do well to recall that fact."

She held her breath as his fingers tightened in her hair, pulling her head back, his eyes tracing the column of her throat.

"I do not fear you." Bede winced at the crack in her voice. Her heart thundered in her ears, echoing the pulse of desire racing along her body. His hot breath danced over her face, and the bristles of his whiskers rasped over her chin. She licked her dry lips, her eyes closing at the coppery tang lingering on his lips. No, it was not fear she felt for the man in front of her. It would be far simpler to fear him.

"Mayhap you should."

Her lips parted with each word, her breathing coming in shallow pants. "Perhaps, milord, it should be you who fears me?"

Gawain's rough chuckle shook his body, the motion forcing him to rub against her hardened nipples. "What's the little mortal going to do? Stab me?" He pulled her head back a little further. "You've tried that, remember?" The bristles of his day old beard tickled along her throat, the slow glide of his hot tongue stirred the spark within her and she swallowed. Her eyes rolled back, and a faint whimper escaped.

Bede willed the tremble in her body away, her nails digging into his skin. "Indeed, and had I realized how much it would pain me to miss, I'd have gone..." She gasped, the breath knocked from her when he pushed her against a tree.

"Bossy, irritating, you've trod upon my nerves from the moment I've met you. Were you anyone else, I'd slit your throat and leave you to rot, wench." Gawain gnashed his teeth at her.

A low chuckle escaped from her lips. His eyes darkened, narrowing, the intent in them clear even to her inexperienced mind. Her breath caught, trapped in her chest with each slow move he made toward her. Licking her lips, she moaned softly at the flare of desire before his mouth crashed into hers, his tongue darting out to trace her lips.

The faint, coppery taste of blood washed over her tongue, along with the heady taste of male. Masterful, his tongue forced its way past her lips, his thumb pulling her chin down so he could breach her defenses. Hot, slick, his tongue dueled with hers. It swept to every corner, intent on conquering each inch of her mouth. She moaned, her body aflame, and he drew back for a moment. Desire mixed with confusion as wave after wave of pleasure swept over her. A tiny cry of dismay filtered through her ragged breathing when his lips left hers. Muttered words soothed her, lips and teeth traced over her jaw, her ear, down her throat. The faint scratch of a fang only added to the heightened senses as he laved and sucked on her pulse.

Heavy, her breasts tightened into aching points when he palmed them. His touch was familiar, knowing. The very lack of hesitancy was enough to prick her fear even as it turned her on. A shudder raced over her at the sensation of a single drop of liquid from a fang sliding down her throat, dipping between her breasts. Each increment of skin the liquid touched flared with desire, awakening her to the pleasures of the flesh. His harsh groan as he arched against her built on the fire between them.

Hands grappled with clothing, pushing it aside, fingers seeking the bare flesh beneath.

Stumbling, Bede panted, her gaze steady on Gawain who stared back at her. The weight of his palm on the curve of her breast seared into her memory. "How…"

"No, I shan't be so careless. Gods above, I took vows." Gawain straightened her blouse, a noticeable tremble in his fingers. "It is best we go."

Her eyes burning with unshed tears, she stared at him. There was no hope of moving until her legs regained their strength. Glancing away from the penetrating heat in his dark eyes, she froze, all desire fading like water from a bottomless bucket.

Slithering across his chest, marred by blood and hair, a multi-colored serpent stared back at her. Its coils wrapped around a dagger, one like the one she carried. The hilt decorated with the flowing red of a ribbon all while engulfed by the massive body of the snake.

"Where did you get this mark?" She reached out to touch him, to trace over the snake, only to jump back when he snapped his teeth at her.

"It is the mark of my clan. My kindred." Gawain pulled the ragged edges of his shirt closed. "Sacred to my kind."

"A vampire with religion?" Bede shook her

head, her mind a tangled mess of thoughts seeming beyond belief. "'Tis not possible. You cannot have such…"

"Cannot have what, milady? Faith or something different than the tales you've obviously been told. Aye, my people have been made out to be monsters who steal children from their beds, sucking them dry, all the while rutting like beasts on any female in sight. 'Tis not me."

"Nay." Bede shook her head, her stomach twisting. Memories stirred, the image of her mother's naked back flickering gold in the firelight. Her mother's eyes glowing with emotion, with rage, the fire slowly ebbing from them with each passing day. "The dagger, why do you have such a mark upon your flesh? It is like my mother's…"

"To hold such a mark… Only those who have served the Queens hold claim to the Dagger…" Gawain paled, his eyes widening as he stepped back. He traced the tattoo decorating his body, his eyes growing vacant before he shook his head, a mask settling in place. "The nearest sorceress is seven nights north of here. Come, we'd best go."

Bede watched him slip into the shadows, confusion settling like a weight about her shoulders. What was he doing here? Gawain had saved her life, and risked his own to save Una—but at what cost?

There had to be an explanation for why this warrior would do so much.

Why would he bear the image of a weapon her mother had passed down to her?

Her hand trembled as it went to the warm metal on her hip. Her fingers tightened around the hilt. "Bede, what have you done?" Her whisper drifted away on the slight breeze, unanswered, leaving Bede with the heavy cloak of loneliness.

Chapter Seven

His skin tight, uncomfortable, Gawain paced the confines of the small cave they'd found. Thick storm clouds and the pouring rain blocked most of the sunlight. The urge to keep moving pulled at him, but it wasn't safe. Every step by the opening made his skin itch.

Gawain braced one hand on the cold stone and stared out through the opening. It made no sense. Why had Anagor taken the babe and left Bede? Anagor was not the kind to seek out children, so someone had to have sent him. But the who eluded him. Hemat wanted the girl - he wanted what she could give him. It was unlikely Hemat would send the sunwalker - Anagor was an outcast, a freak. One any vampire worth their blood would hunt.

So who else wanted the child - and for what?

Wincing at the sharp bite of pain through his fangs, Gawain glanced behind him. At the back of the cave, tucked up against the stone wall, Bede curled into the fetal position on the ground, the tattered remains of her clothing peering from beneath the dark leather of his cloak. Her dark hair was tangled with debris and matted blood, the strands spilled across the ground. Bruises marred the thin skin beneath her eyes, the harsh finger prints along her throat and arms stark in their coloration. Under her skin the pale blue lines of her veins stood out in stark relief.

"Nay, I'm not Dorstan or Anagor. I'll not damn both of our eternal souls to Stylox by drinking from a woman." He strode to the back of the cave, sinking to the ground, one booted foot braced against the damp stone. The air around him smelled of rain, clean, fresh…like the sleeping woman. He inhaled, his body tensing at the faint but familiar perfume of her that teased his nose. He looked at Bede, images floating across his mind's eye, blurring her visage and setting his blood to boiling.

"No. Gods above, no." Screams of anguish rose above the din of battle as Gawain raced up the stairs. Dread settled like chains about his ankles as he pushed past dragons, past demons, ruthlessly killing to get to his king. Slamming through the broken chamber doors, his sword clattered to the stone beneath his feet.

Blood dripped from the pale beard of a general. His red eyes narrowed with delight as he licked the blood from his lips. At his feet, her elegant body broken, her eyes staring sightlessly at nothing, lay his queen, the one he'd sworn on all that was holy to protect.

"No." Sinking to his knees, Gawain stared at the bloody corpse, anger like a tidal wave growing within him to slam through the defenses of his control. Rage swarmed over him, giving him strength as he launched himself across the room. Saltar's merciless laughter filled the air as he swung his sword to block Gawain's attack. Ducking beneath the heavy blade, Gawain sank his axe into Saltar's leg, nearly severing it as the old vampire fell, screaming in agony.

"Nay, Gawain." Hema's shocked voice halted his blade. "Death is too good." He paused, his eyes narrowing to glow a dangerous scarlet as they settled on Saltar's bloody face. "How could you? You, my most trusted general, my friend. You have betrayed me in a manner most foul. Be it a curse upon you! A curse upon those who are of your ilk, of your clan! No more shall you be free."

Gawain jerked from the memories, his gaze falling on the sleeping woman as his hand traced over the long, jagged scar down his face. It was the mark he wore since that night. A sign of his failure—a blow given by Saltar.

Rising, his emotions swinging wildly, he palmed his chest. Hemat had not accused, nor blamed— but that had not done much to dissuade others.

Now, it was like he'd been thrown from his clan, his cast. How he wished he could go back, save the beautiful dracvipen and regain what his fellow warriors had shunned him for. Shaking his head, he turned to pace back through the darkness. Recriminations and regrets would only weigh him down.

A soft moan from behind him drew along his body like a string. The faint note of arousal, of want, enough to stroke his cock and build a fire within him. His fangs lengthened, sharpened, the tips aching with a different need…a different hunger flowed through his blood. He closed his eyes, the images burning through his mind.

The pale curve of a hip, the swell of a breast as he drew the hardened nipple into his mouth, his fangs tracing over it. The heady scent of her sweet blood beneath the flesh flooding his senses as he nibbled on her neck. Her muted cry as she came around his fingers, his fangs sunk deep into where her shoulder and neck joined.

"Gawain!" Bede's sharp tone ripped him from his thoughts. He straightened, his hand already reaching for his sword at the sheer terror within her voice. Beyond her, he caught the faint movement of a shadow and any hint of arousal was scorched away by pure rage.

Gawain leapt to his feet and strode forward, putting himself between the intruder and Bede.

"Captain, what do you want?" Gawain eased the sword from its sheath, one hand darting out to toss Bede behind him.

"I warned our king you were not the one to send on such a mission. Yet he still sends you. Pity. I come seeking–"

"I certainly hope it isn't the woman. I've little patience for those who would steal from me— even if they do have Hemat's ear."

"Why would I concern myself with the wench?" His lips twisted into a sneer, Dorstan stepped from the shadows. "I've a dozen waiting to warm my bed at any moment. Women who are far more beautiful than this simple *human*. They understand all the needs of a man. She is as untutored as a stone, and I've no desire to be her instructor."

"Perhaps then you should go stalk them. Or are you hunting?" Gawain ground out. His palms sweaty, Gawain narrowed his eyes. Surely Dorstan would not be so foolish to attempt to hunt his prey. Anger and fear warred within his chest and he stepped forward. "I've not seen a single dragon of late nor any dhymphur."

Dorstan's eyes flashed and he bared his teeth. "Gawain, you're favored by the king, 'tis the only reason you still live. You should have died six hundred years before this night. Sadly, you did not, and now you walk a line the king has drawn,"

Dorstan hissed. "I come because Hemat has ordered it. I bear a warning for you."

"Warning? Ah perhaps you have already whispered into his ear of my apparent misstep." Gawain felt his stomach drop. Could it be that Dorstan had sent Anagor? The vampire Captain was not above such a thing. "Has King Hemat decided my failure to secure the babe is worthy of note? How could I be so foolish to let one get—"

"He has no knowledge of the girl's disappearance. Rather there is danger on the wind. General Saltar has stirred. Someone has loosened his bonds in Norech. There are still some who are loyal to the bastard. One of his servants attacked a small village—slaughtered many before he was driven off by a demoness and her minions. Hemat has sent an envoy to her to seek terms."

"The demoness holds the villagers captive? What terms could she possible have? Hemat must send—"

"She holds no one. It is rumored that she is a warrior priestess, serves Nerafail, one of his cursed. Phantalia says her fate lies with One of the Seven."

"Demons? Saltar? What blasphemy is this?" Bede clung to Gawain's arm, doubt a thread in her croaked words.

"My, my, my, the little fleshling speaks. I would have believed he'd have bit out your tongue by now. Though, goodness me, I see no marks upon that lovely neck. What's the matter, Gawain? Not tempting enough for you? She is not the one Hemat seeks, drink of her and discard the husk. You have a duty…"

His stomach twisted and flames licked at the edge of his vision. A rumbling growl echoed in the cave and he stepped forward. "Do not challenge me, Dorstan," Gawain snarled. His fangs lengthened, sharpening menacingly. His claws flared, glinting in the weak light. "My vows hold true, unlike yours. You seek the enemy, slaughtering the young when you should be focusing instead on securing our king's line."

"Mind me, warrior, find the girl. Return her to the king's court so that your honor will be recovered. I've no desire to drift from our realm to this one without just reasoning."

"How did you get here?" Gawain pressed the tip of his blade against Dorstan's throat. "There are no portals here. I would sense a gatekeeper if there were."

"Really, Gawain, you are so foolish. There is no need—"

"Did you follow me from three suns past? Or perhaps you came before I did. Tell me, how is it that you came to be here? Perhaps you're working with Anagor to seize the prize before I can deliver her to our king. The lizard killer and the sunwalker, how trite. How traitorous." He licked at the tip of a fang, tasting the bitter venom that formed, the anger that coursed through at the subtle challenge that came from within the ranks of his sect.

"I've no need to travel by portal." Dorstan eyed Bede for a moment, his eyes flashing before he turned and stepped out into the storm. "Find the babe, his lordship has plans for her."

"No, Gawain, you cannot—"

"Be silent, woman." Dorstan's furious hiss filled the cave as he shimmered in the rain. "Your pathetic desires have no meaning to us. Kill the bitch and find the babe, and do it with all due haste."

Gawain roared in fury with the flash of Dorstan's disappearance. His nails bit into his palms, his fangs aching with the desire to kill. Whirling, he glared at Bede who stepped back, her breathing fast, shallow, terror in her eyes. Yet he didn't sense it directed at him. Nay, it was something far deeper, far more sinister that she feared.

"Calm yourself, Bede, I've no desire…" He trailed off at the desperate shake of her head. Confusion clouded his mind for a moment before she spoke.

"I can smell it." Bede's soft whisper was like a slap. "Fire, blood. It is deeper, richer…"

Shock ripped into him, and his jaw dropped. It was impossible, no mortal could smell what he had long since grown accustomed to. The hot metallic scent, the hiss of ancient blood cooling within a body. "What is this you smell?"

"Blood boiling over a fire. Wood, smoke, I can taste it on my tongue. Sweet yet bitter, it congeals but never loses its scent." Tears filled her eyes as she pressed fingers to her lips. "It is unlike anything I've ever smelt. Living almost. It lies on my tongue as though I'd gorged myself upon it recently."

Gawain strode to the cave opening and stared out. "'Tis the odor of a dragon. You should not scent such a thing. There has been no dragon seen here. We are at…" He froze, ice flowing through his veins. "That is how he came to be here. He has forsaken it all. He drank of them, 'tis why he is so feared upon the battlefield. His thirst for dragon blood has made him a slave to his desires."

"Milord?"

Turning at Bede's hesitant query he narrowed his eyes, his fangs easing a bit. "How is it you scented him? None but those living within the clan have done so in centuries. What manner of fleshling are you?" His fist tangled in her hair, pulling her closer, the scent of her blood filling his nose. Sweet, innocent, it battered the chastity he'd embraced for so many years.

Staring at her, he felt something snap, like a broken bone that had been set, and realization hit. Aye, she was one of *them*—one of Saltar's line–and she belonged to him.

The enemy was within his grasp.

Revenge would be sweet.

* * * *

"Gawain, what did he mean? What use could your king have with my sister?" His eyes flashed red, broiling with emotion before he took a step back. Bede shuddered, something within her recoiling into a small, hard ball of ice. She swallowed and exhaled a shaky breath. "Gawain?"

Gawain waved a hand to halt her. "It is your line. Long ago, your leader betrayed his people, our people. He did not simply break every vow there was, he shattered them and then pissed on the broken shards of his hone. King Hemat condemned both him and his followers. Your sister is in some way important to keeping that traitor locked within his prison." Gawain sheathed his sword with a quick, rough motion. "I was not made privy to the king's thoughts, but I would guess his intent. He seeks to discover the truth about her, to use the gifts she has been given, and use that power to keep Saltar bound."

"Milord, I do not see…"

"See? See what?" Gawain snarled in her face. Beneath the anger, a faint spark shifted and Bede felt the slow glide of scales beneath her skin. His words were sharp, like a dagger to her heart and she longed to halt him from continuing. "You are disposable, Bede, a fleshling with nothing more than blood flowing through your veins. 'Tis not you my king sent me to retrieve…"

"He's going to kill her, isn't he?" Bede raked a hand through her hair. "Just as you are going to kill me. It is what your commander ordered you to do. It is my end, my sister's end—"

"I have no interest in your death. Nor do I see the death of your Una, but I do not know." Gawain adjusted his cloak and eyed the sky. "It is not for me to say. Come, we haven't much time and I wish to be as far from here as we can get before the sun rises."

"My poor Una." Her mind whirled, racing from thought to thought. She needed to keep her sister safe, but how? How could she, a mortal woman, keep these animals from slaughtering Una? She rubbed at her eyes to clear the burning sensation.

He wrapped his hand around her arm, the soft touch at odds with his harsh tone. Her eyes flew to his and her heart stuttered, shocked at the pain, the remorse within his dark eyes.

"Come, Bede. We must go."

****

Like air from a bladder, the hiss filled her head. Shimmering along the pale flesh of his throat, its golden eyes glowed. With each pulse of her heart, the serpent unfurled his hood, spreading, wrapping around his throat until its forked tongue licked at the corner of his lips. Scales rasped along the stubble of his jaw.

Its slender body slithered along his torso. A single drop of crimson blood clung to its tail as it wrapped around where his heart would be. Each breath he took spread the hood, the snake rising from the flesh until it was a living, breathing entity.

"'Tis not possible."

"Certainly, it is." The snake's voice filled her mind. "Just as it must be." Separating from Gawain's body, it danced in the air, inching off his flesh until it began wrapping itself around her. "Why do you deny what is yours by right, Bede? Why do you not claim what you hold? He is yours. As you are his. Honor will bind you long after the fear has faded. Come, look upon yourself and see."

Pulled by some invisible thread, her hand clinging to Gawain's, they slipped along the rocky shore to the water. Staring down into the clear water, Bede's eyes widened at the image that greeted her. Hovering over her shoulder, the snake flicked its tongue out and in. Tasting, smelling—she cared not. Along her throat, itching, burning, ripping through the tender skin, another being fought. Its fangs and claws shredding skin until it too coiled around her throat, its vibrant blue hue at odds with the darkened gray of Gawain's snake.

"No! This cannot be." Bede grabbed at her throat, the tickle of a tongue flicking out, dancing across her palm. "I...I..."

"It is done. We are one, together there is no danger." The snake whispered in her ear as he wound around her until he was side by side with the image on her throat. She cried softly at the tearing sensation as the blue serpent unwound from her neck to slither along her flesh, down her arm, and sink its fangs into Gawain's body.

"No! Please, he..."

"Shh." Gawain cupped her jaw. "'Tis done. One cannot take without giving, Bede. The man may doubt, but we cannot." His voice lowered as the snakes danced along their bodies, pulling and twisting until they were pressed together. Only then did they seem to crawl beneath their flesh and vanish, leaving her with a strange urge to scratch her neck…and an even stronger urge to sink her teeth into the spot between his shoulders and neck that screamed at her instincts to take.

****

Shaken, her mouth gaping open, Bede stared at Gawain's retreating figure. Her hand reached up, her fingertips trailing over the raised welt at her throat. She didn't need a reflection to know it was the dripping fangs of a serpent.

Chapter Eight

Dorstan's arrival had proven to be a distraction, one that had far more dangerous results. How was it that a mortal was aware of who or what Dorstan was when his own kind had little idea? Gawain adjusted the weight of the woodland creature he'd caught and strode into the shadows along the edge of their camp.

The gods played with them. Delivering his enemy into his care and making her his fated one. He had no time for such frivolity.

Gawain dropped the carcass next to the small fire and glanced at Bede. Her eyes were closed, lips parted, one arm stretched out. His cloak covered her, the leather molding to her gentle curves. Beneath the grime and pale flesh, the soft thud of her pulse reached his ears.

He inhaled, sweet, heady, her arousal filled her scent, plucking at his control like a well-meaning child with a toy.

His fangs aching, he growled. How long would he be able to control the desire racing through him? What would it feel like to claim her, to dive into her and slake the hunger making his cock ache? She'd be sweeter than fresh blood. Tight, fitting him like a glove, her hips undulating beneath his, her breasts filling his palms. Confusion tangled with lust, irritating him further.

He palmed his shaft through the leather of his trews. Embers flared, his blood heated as his cock twitched. Gods above, why would she be the one to stir him to life? Was it not enough he had failed his queen - but to be offered a treasure... nay, he hissed at the writhing coil in his gut. Pleasure unlike nothing he'd ever known ripped through him. Turning, he strode from the firelight, certain a bit of distance would soothe the fire raging in his loins.

Remember your vow, Gawain. It must not be broken, no matter the temptation.

The hilt of his sword felt good in his hand as his eyes scanned the shadows. He needed to rid himself of these urges. It was too dangerous for both of them.

She was mortal, human, basic food for some of his kind. Dorstan and his ilk would take delight in drinking from her tender neck. They would wallow in the sweetness of her blood, even as they– His fangs ached at the mere thought of another drinking from her. Slashing through the air, he growled at the branch that landed at his feet. "Food never looked this good." Gawain kicked at the fallen wood. Impassively, he watched it scratch and skip across the dirt, disturbing the foliage upon the ground.

Tension filled his body at the softest of rustles. The leaves began to shift, to move, the warm, earthy scent of a reptile flooding upward. He tongued a fang as the small glowing eyes peered from the blanket of fallen leaves.

Leaves rustled over scales, the foliage moving around him.

"Gawain!" Soft, the feminine voice washed over him, the tone soothing. The leaves shifted beneath his feet, and scales rasped over each other as the beast coiled, its long, mute-hued body brushing against his ankles. "You have spent a lifetime honoring me. Great is your tribute but I did not mean your vows to be a prison. Aye, my son, you offer your sword, your blood, your heart, and yet you forget service is something freely given. You hide behind your vows, wearing them as you would armor. Yet you have forgotten much."

Striking out at the serpent, Gawain snarled in fury as it simply coiled away from him, lifted its head, and flicked its tongue toward the fire. "What nonsense do you speak? You know nothing of who I am or what vows I've taken. Show yourself, sorceress!" Gawain whirled, his sword flashing in the fading light.

Dull throbbing raced along his fingers, the slow crawl of his claws sliding forward tugging on nerves rarely used. Acrid and bitter liquid coated his tongue. His fangs dug into his lips. Gawain spun wildly, his gaze darting through the trees.

Fear filled him, as bitter as dead blood, when his eyes fell on *his* female.

Bede slept on, her body curled around his cloak, her hand pressed against her abdomen, her breasts rising and falling with each breath.

"Show yourself, coward. Or haven't you the stomach to face me?" Gawain growled. In a whirl of smoke and dust, he teleported, his booted feet braced next to where Bede lay so peacefully. The need to protect her stronger than anything he'd ever known, stronger than the need to feed...within her lay power, pure, sweet, and it was *his*.

Sword in hand, his eyes scanned the forest floor. The wind whistled through the branches, playing a soft melody. Each note clearer in his ears than ever before. In the distance, the haunting howl of a wolf answered by its mate. Faint, the odor of bodies, of men filtered through the night air, through the distance. Their blood rank with liquor and rancor.

"I am of no danger to her, Gawain." The flames shifted, dancing upward before being extinguished. Pale blue ones rose into the night, waltzing around the full-busted woman who stared at him from within their flickering depths. "So young, were you not? Eager to embrace the calling, to forsake everything but your duty to your queen. Forsaking love itself before you knew its power." Dark eyes stared from a pale face, the voluptuous curves wrapped in a sheer fabric that fluttered within the fire.

"Leave her." Gawain rolled his sword. Using it as a lance, he tossed it. The weapon clattered to the stony ground beyond the woman. Frustration boiled, it seemed he could do nothing to rid himself of the witch. "She is of no consequence to you. Go back to that whore you serve and leave her and I in peace. It will be your only warning, witch."

Orange and purple flared within the flames before they settled into the gentle flow of blues and whites. "If you mean to say—"

"Go back to Amuliana, tell her I have no use for her servants or her slaves." Gawain shifted, slashing at the woman with his claws. "I do not serve—" She shifted back, his claws slicing through the air in front of her body.

"Neither of us do, Gawain. You are a man of honor. She is a weak-willed whore who craves the bounties of the flesh. My name and hers will never be spoken as anything but enemies."

"And yet here you are."

"Ah, here for you. For her." She gestured to

Bede. "She is of us. Of you." The woman smiled, her fingers beckoning Gawain closer. She reached for him, her grip firm, unbreakable as she took his arm and turned him to face Bede's sleeping figure. "Look upon her, Gawain. Look and tell me you do not feel it. Feel that need that burns within you. It hardens your shaft, fills you with power, with a hunger you've never known. Only within her will the need be slaked. The thirst be quenched. Within your mate, you will find power unlike any you can imagine—and a redemption not even Amuliana can seize from you. Hear my words, my son, follow the heart beating within your chest as it guides you to the one you desire above all others."

"Please, I beg of thee, let her be. Punish me. Punish my weakness, not her." Gawain struggled within the woman's grasp. "She does not deserve to bear the weight of all of my sins."

"Punish?" The woman chuckled. "Weakness? Of all my warriors, you have proven to be the most resilient. The one who most closely embraced your guilt, your shame at the death of your beloved queen. For all that King Hemat has railed against you, for all the failures you think you have done, you are the one least deserving of such a penance. You did not betray her, Gawain. The betrayal came from another."

"I shirked my duty."

"For years now, I have watched you punish

97

yourself, wallow in your guilt. Unlike others of your sect, of your kind, you still choose to wear the scars of that night. Your soul is burdened not by failure, Gawain, but your self imposed exile. Condemning yourself will not undo what was done. It is time you step from the shadows, from the fears, the horror and grief Hemat still clings to. Be at peace, embrace your future. Gawain, you are more than a guard for the queen. You are a man of honor, of intent. The last of an order many thought dead long ago. One that some wish had fallen away long before you took your vows." She turned him, her face pressing against his with an icy touch.

"My king has a far different view than yours, milady." Gawain ground out through clenched teeth. "He would—"

"Hemat is a man who will learn in time that he is wrong." Her claws dug into his skin. "In his grief and rage he has committed as foul an act as Saltar did. My children are not meant to be apart - they are not meant to be shunned and starved. Nay, Gawain, Hemat, King of the Vampire will learn in time. For now, you must understand the gift you would run away from."

"I would not condemn Bede to a fate—"

"She is yours." She pointed a delicate finger.

Gawain groaned in protest. It could not be. He wasn't worthy of such a gift, of such honor. His stomach dropped to his feet and he shook his head. "It is too fine a gift. She is mortal, and far too fine for my world, Goddess."

Soft laughter danced across the wind and Gawain gaped as the serpent slithered up and over Bede's sleeping form. The thin red fork of its tongue caressed her cheek, its lips seeping to pull back from his teeth. Gawain stared in horror as the snake coiled over her. It reared up, its hood extended, the glowing slits of its eyes focusing on him with each passing heartbeat.

Its jaws open, long, hollow fangs dropped, dripping the acidic fluid. The serpent sunk its dripping fangs deep within Bede's flesh. Thin red lines raced along her throat toward her breasts as the venom pumped through her blood.

"No." Gawain trembled, his flesh crawling as his tattoo shifted, the scales rasping as his beast stirred. "She cannot... You cannot mean to..."

"I do mean." The flames flickered white. "You have honored your vow, your life has been spent protecting, serving. With her by your side, your power will be limitless. It pains me to see my children under threat. Only through victory can peace be found. Embrace her, Gawain, take joy the life you were destined for." In a shower of sparks the woman seemed to vanish, her companion fading away in a dissipating mist. "Beware, Gawain, of the one who wears two faces. Look not at the old enemy but to a new foe. For in that foe you will find the greatest threat."

A shudder raced through him as his sword flew with a flick of her wrist to land at his feet. His ears filled with the throbbing pulse of life. "I will not break my vow." Somehow, his whispered promise sounded hollow as if he'd already broken it. "Selene, be merciful, I pray to thee, do not curse her with the weight of my sins."

Chapter Nine

Bede shifted, the muted voices penetrating the stillness in her mind. A familiar rumble melted into the delicate cadence of a feminine voice. One that was oddly recognizable. It couldn't be.

She pushed herself up into a sitting position and glanced around. The fire had burnt down to embers, casting barely enough light to see the carcass laying next to it. Shadows moved along the edge of her vision and she twisted around. Gawain's figure lurked by the fire, the faint odor of flowers and ash clung to the air. So the same woman had been there.

Bede gathered herself and climbed to her feet. The fabric of her shift brushed against her sensitive breasts, hardening her nipples until they ached. Heavy, the longing flowed like wine through her blood. Hissing she hunched over as she walked. If only she could recall what she'd been dreaming of.

Gawain stood, lips pulled back, teeth bared, a look of rage twisting his face into a terrifying mask. The long, ugly scar was white with the force of his emotional turmoil.

She paused, a strange calm seeping like a chill into her. There was no fear, no hesitation. Instead, she could feel an answering darkness building. Like ants beneath her skin, the flesh along her neck crawled. She scratched at the sensitive skin, her nails digging into the tender flesh of her throat; the sensation streaking through her. Ignoring the faint, uncertain whisper at the back of her mind, Bede reached out.

Looking at him through her lashes, she took his wrist. Dark eyes followed her every move as she nuzzled into his palm, her tongue darting out to lick at the flesh. Heat flared, scorching along her nerve endings with each whimper, each growl. Shock, awareness, and lust lit his gaze as her fingers tightened, nails digging in, creating furrows with each attempted withdrawal of his hand.

Her mouth ached, her teeth throbbing, Bede licked along her teeth, whimpering at the slow stroke of her tongue over the sharp point of an incisor. She met his hard stare, her lips curling upward a moment before she bared her teeth. His growl drowned his muted protest as she sank her teeth deep into the tender flesh between his index finger and thumb. She quivered at the rush of power, of sheer pleasure that poured over her with the first drops of blood on her tongue.

"No." Gawain's hand tangled in her hair, sharp pain lancing through her when he jerked her head back. "Bede, you cannot. Gods…" he hissed with the movement of her jaw as she lapped at the wound.

Digging her nails deeper, Bede pushed her hand

up his body, tangling her fingers in the laces of his tunic. Humming softly, she let go, her tongue tracing over her lips to lap at the warm blood lingering there. "I can." She leaned closer, her attention on the faint lines beneath his skin.

"Woman, this is not what you desire," Gawain ground out. "It is only the serpent's bite, a trick by those who would toy with your fate."

"I think not." Bede trailed a finger down his throat, marveling at the subtle shift of flesh, the darkening of the lines. "I dreamt this. Dreamt of your touch, your fire. Why would I doubt what I have—"

"What more did you dream of?" Gawain jerked her closer, his eyes narrowing. "Quickly, speak up. Perhaps it was not the child I was…"

Bede struggled within his grasp at the reminder of Una. Oh gods, how had she forgotten her sister? Gods she was cursed and a fool. Una was innocent, a child. "My sister, Una, we must…" Bede's voice cracked.

"And we shall. Tell me all of your dreams, Bede." Gawain cupped her jaw, his voice filled with urgency. His eyes swept her face, heat and fear tangled within the depths with each passing heartbeat.

"There are so many." Bede shivered, her lashes

falling.

"Have you dreamt of the one who wears a false face?"

Bede stiffened at the urgency, the raw emotion in his voice. Her mind scrambled, images flashed before her. "Nay." Her voice broke. "I dreamt of you most of late. Snakes, aye, I've dreamt of mating snakes wrapping around us, their bodies sliding over our skin, their eyes glowing." She stared, shocked, as the pallor vanished from his skin, turning it translucent. What could shock the warrior before her?

"When did you dream this?" Gawain's grip tightened painfully.

Tugging on his wrist, she broke free. Bede stumbled back, her body on fire. Every nerve burning, her skin pulled tight, her heart galloping beneath her ribs.

"Two days past, milord. After we saw the man in the cave, I had the vision, saw the snakes come alive, their fangs flashing. Aye, they spoke to me. Their voices were seductive, easing my fears. Embracing me, embracing us as they mated beneath our flesh."

"'Tis true then." Gawain stepped back, his eyes closed. "Goddess, you challenge my strength, I cannot break my vow. It is what protects us all."

Bede frowned at the torment in his words. "Vow, milord? You make no sense." Gasping when he whirled, his fingers grabbing her hair, Bede gaped at him. Longing warred with fear, and she could not decide which she prayed most to win.

"We are but half a night's ride from one who can direct us to a portal. We will seek her council. I will find Una. You will be safe until my return. I must know why she would tempt me with what she knows to be forbidden."

"Who?"

"I cannot say." Gawain nearly sobbed, his body tense, his eyes darting wildly rather than meeting hers. "The trees have ears and loosened tongues. Come, douse the flames. If we ride hard, we will be in her realm long before the sun rises."

Bede watched Gawain vanish into the shadows, the snorts of the horses loud in the silence. What vow had he made that he was being tempted to break?

More importantly, how would he react when he knew just how futile it was to fight what the goddess had told her - and the fire burning between them?

Chapter Ten

Her backside aching, Bede shifted in the saddle. Hours of riding and still they were no closer to wherever or whoever Gawain sought to be. Around them, the thick foliage and tall spruce pressed in like walls to keep them on the narrow road. The very air was close, too close, it clogged in her throat and choked her.

Gods above she was eager to be done with all of it.

A subtle shift in the wind carried the faint trace of something. Her stomach rumbled and she took a deep breath. Sharp like vinegar it mixed with the raw, earthy scent of sweat, and the rancidness of unwashed bodies. It settled like a blanket around her teasing her senses. Her gums aching, she pressed her tongue to the sharp point of one tooth. The ache eased, blending into the dull throb of her heartbeat. What was she becoming?

Figures moved in front of them, her horse snorting and sidestepping beneath her. Six men gathered in the road. Threadbare clothing hung from their boney frames. The stench of sweat and disease rolled into the biting hint of lust, anger, and rage.

"Gawain?" Nudging her mount closer to him, she stifled a shudder when one of the men stepped forward, his eyes narrowed, saliva pooling at the corners of his mouth as he stared at her.

"They'll not touch you." Fury laced through his voice, drowned only by the singing of metal against metal. Moonlight gleamed, dancing off the blade as he swung off his horse and pushed the animal's head aside. "Let us pass and perhaps I shall let you continue your wretched existence."

"We got needs, wants…" The obvious spokesman of the group scratched at his beard. Taller than the others by a head, his long scraggly hair fell past his shoulders. Faded red rags clung to his body. At his side, the short, broad blade of a sword seemed out of place in his hand. He grinned, what remained of his teeth were broken or blackened.

The other men gathered behind him, their hands upon their weapons in a clear statement of intent.

"Speak your terms, parasite, and be done with it," Gawain hissed.

"The horses, the gold." The man paused, his tongue licking obscenely at his lips. "Your whore."

"The lady…well, she is mine." Gawain's posture changed, his shoulders tensed, legs spread to brace his weight. Bede shuddered at the flash of his claws. She leaned forward, bracing her weight against the horse's withers. Death would come for them - and she would be ready. Bede licked her lips, her stomach twisting, a gnawing ache settled beneath her heart. A feast laid out before her. Aye, there would be bloodshed.

"Move out of our path." His voice shook with malice, the faint scent of his rage bubbling along the wind to her.

"Gawain?"

"Bede, have no fear. I'll not let them—"

"Come, just give us what we want and save yourself the hurt you'll endure if you don't. You have so much, we have so little." The group snickered, spreading out to blatantly challenge them.

"Get out of our way. Humans. So eager to inflict pain and suffering upon each other. To harm those they should treasure. Remove yourselves from our path or die where you stand." Gawain vibrated with rage, his voice dark, a thread of danger that sent a bolt of unease up Bede's spine.

Bede gasped as the highwaymen lunged forward, clubs and swords at the ready. The air reverberated with the clash of weapons as they attacked. Blades swung wildly, cutting into soft flesh, breaking bone after bone. Screams of agony and terror filled the air. An outlaw landed on the ground in front of the horses, his body mangled, eyes staring sightlessly into the night sky. The horses screamed in terror, bolting from the trail. Losing her grip on the reins, Bede landed hard, her breath knocked from her lungs. Scrambling to her feet, she swallowed against the growing lump in her throat.

Fear tangled with a darker, deadlier instinct when one man darted past Gawain, his beady eyes narrowed, a wild, crazed look in them. Anger flared, like a freshly poked fire. Fear faded, a cold instinct settling over her as she drew her dagger and stepped back. She squinted at him and licked her lips, her stomach turning when her assailant followed the movement, his lips curling up to reveal rotted teeth.

He lunged forward, his fingers ripping at the smock she wore. Disgust rolled her stomach as his filthy flesh touched hers. Her dagger burned against her palm. *Kill him. You can, you must. Protect your mate.*

Power lurched in her stomach at the faint metallic taste on her tongue when he punched her. Stumbling back a half a step, she eyed him with cold disdain, the tip of her blade flashing in the moonlight. Instinct and hunger roared through her. With an icy fascination she focused on the wretch before her. Shock grabbed her at the scratch of a fang over her tongue. Acrid, rancid, the stench of blood filled her nose as she watched her blade slide through the flesh of the man before her. A red tidal wave flowed down his throat, staining his clothes, and he fell to his knees, shock, horror, and a strange relief in his eyes.

Her heart racing, she watched him collapse into a heap at her feet, her stomach rumbling. Gawain's agonized roar drew her attention. Mobbed, Gawain was struggling with the men swarming over him. She gnashed her teeth together at the sight of a blade sticking from his body. Three cowards rushed at him, their weapons forgotten, their fists and feet crashing into him again and again. Their relentless attack pushed Gawain back, away from her. Away from the safety she offered.

A haze of red filled her vision. Rage crashed through her, a storm of unimagined power and fury lashing at her control. With a deep, vicious snarl that drew the attention of one, she lurched forward. Her nails scored his flesh, drawing blood as she grabbed a hold. The need to sink her teeth into his flesh pulled her closer and closer to the brink. A strange ache filled her mouth, her tongue swollen, saliva dripping as she pulled his head back.

With a scream of primal emotion, Bede sunk her teeth deep. The flesh gave way like the crust on a loaf of bread. Each pull on the bittersweet liquid filled her with a sense of purpose, a hunger she'd never felt. The man beneath her squirmed, screamed, and clawed at the earth, his voice garbled with each passing second.

"Help me!" His fingers scratched into the dirt, raking up leaves.

Bede wretched his head back, the sound of bones crunching leaving her with a sense of satisfaction. Tossing him in a twitching heap on the ground, she turned her attention to the others. The rancid stench of fear filled her head as she appraised them beneath her lashes. Her stare penetrated each of them, and she felt her lips curl. Licking her lips, she moaned softly at the faint traces of blood clinging to her flesh before rising to her feet.

She slipped her toe beneath the hilt of a sword and sent it flying into the air. She caught it skillfully. Spinning it in her palm, she advanced. "Cowards, befouled insects that prey upon those you believe to be weaker. He is mine, and I care not for your presence."

Throwing the sword, the sickening squelch of it rocking back and forth in the man's flesh drew a strange giddy laugh from her. Bede forward, she caught another in her hands, her nails digging into his throat, blood oozing down his flesh as she pulled him closer. The remaining bandits scrambled, screaming into the darkness.

Wrinkling her nose at the acidic stench of urine, Bede glanced down to where the man she was holding shook. "Weak. Pathetic. Coward. My baby sister holds more bravery than you. Die, you worthless bag of bones. Aye, you were warned, you should have heeded it and let us pass." Issuing a furious growl, she threw him. His body crashed into a tree and fell with a dull thud to the ground, already forgotten.

Kneeling next to Gawain who groaned in agony, Bede hesitated to touch him. Blood flowed from his chest, soaking his clothing and the ground around her knees. Every nerve in her body ached, a strange craving she'd never known flowing like fire through her veins. Leaning closer, she licked at the wounds on his face, the taste of his blood stirring a fire in her loins.

"No," Gawain protested weakly. "You must not."

"I must," Bede replied, bending forward, her gaze steady. As if someone hovered by her shoulder, whispering the words, she knew what it would take for him to heal, to be strong enough to continue on. "You need to feed. To heal you need blood. There is naught but mine and I would give it gladly."

"I will heal…" Gawain coughed, a splatter of red froth on his lips.

"Aye, but it will take time. Time you do not have." Bede pressed her lips to his face, tracing wound after wound. Sitting back on her haunches, she stared into his pain-filled gaze. "I am sorry." Wincing, she pulled the sword from his chest, tossing it aside without a care.

She squeezed his hand as he roared his agony and fury to the night. There would be no rest tonight, there could be none. Smoothing her hands down his chest, her eyes burned with unshed tears she refused to allow to fall. The time for tears, for fragility, would come, but not in the dirt and blood soaked mud of a battlefield.

"Tell me how I can assist your healing. What do you need to—"

"Blood, fresh blood." Gawain, panting, rolled over to cough. His entire body shaking with the force.

Bede wrinkled her nose at the clots that landed with a splunk before her knees.

He was healing, but time was not on their side. They were in danger here, the enemy would regroup. Perhaps there would be more attackers, perhaps even a Roman legion or two would be out and about. Licking her lips, she glanced around. The road was clear of all signs of the men. Only the man she'd bled remained. Narrowing her eyes, she looked deeper into the forest to the man she'd thrown.

"Did he live?"

"No, there is no heartbeat." Gawain groaned a harsh, agonized sound reaching deep into her very soul. "We cannot remain. Get the horses."

Bede gasped at the touch of his hand. Her eyes widened, and the fire coursing through her veins throbbed to life. Heavy, full, her breasts ached beneath the fabric of her dress. She could feel a hollow throb between her legs, a hunger building. Her eyes darted to his, and she recognized the feelings in his gaze. Lust flared, hotter, stronger than any desire to feed any morality. Leaning closer, she trailed a finger down his face, her nail gathering blood.

Slowly, her eyes locked to his, she lifted her bloody nail to her lips and sucked, a moan of pleasure echoing on the night. His eyes darkened, lips curling up to reveal his extended fangs. The pounding of his blood echoed in her head.

"Yes." Gawain's guttural reply vibrated through her body.

With a groan, she grabbed the front of his tunic, her lips crashing into his. Clumsy, untutored, her tongue traced over his lips, demanding entrance. When he gasped she took full advantage, her tongue darting past his teeth to duel with his.

Scrambling closer, she pressed against him, her hands tangling in his hair, tracing his shoulders, his neck. Again and again she kissed him. Her body on fire, shuddering and moaning with each response from him. Her blood pooling with each caress, each brush of his tongue against hers.

"Gawain, please…" Whimpering, she threw her head back, exposing her throat, desperate for him to sink his teeth into the flesh there. Pressing his head downward, she guided him toward the throbbing pulse of her life's blood.

"Nay, nay, we cannot." Gawain licked, suckled, his muted protest at odds with the way his hands palmed her breasts, teasing her nipples into hardened peaks. "Bede, stop. Gods above, stop me…"

"No, take. Drink." Bede reached up to scratch at her throat. "Take what you need. I am yours." Screaming in pleasure, she shook when he sank his teeth deep. Her body trembling, every nerve alive, the pain bordered on pleasure and she writhed against him. "Yes!"

Pressing closer, she licked her lips, her head shifting, resting against his shoulder. Her hand darted down his body, her fingers seeking the waistband of his trews. His fingers, rough and calloused, grabbed hers as she palmed his hardened cock.

"Nooo, let me." She whimpered, her eyes rolling back in her head as darkness swam within her vision. Each pull on her throat echoed in her womb, and she hovered on the brink. Clinging to him, she pressed closer, tighter, the need to share beyond any control she had.

Stars exploded behind her eyelids as he lapped at the blood oozing from the wound. Already she could feel her body hovering, waiting on the precipice. She flew apart when his fingers touched her bare skin, the nails scoring the insides of her thighs before he cupped her womanhood. Arching her hips into his palm, the friction against her clit shattered her. Screaming out his name, Bede fell into the darkness that hovered around her. Whole, fulfilled for the first time in her life.

Chapter Eleven

Her blood pulsing through her body, Bede followed Gawain through the shadows. The horses had vanished, driven off by fear. Beneath the thin veil of skin, she could hear the whooshing of her own blood. The throbbing of her heart sounded against her ribs. Every sound roared in her ears — the howl of a wolf and the sound of the leaves in the trees. A glance up revealed a world of shadows and darkness, but her eyes could see the indents in the bark of the trees, counting the branches on trees far ahead.

It was as if the gods had blessed her with an endless supply of energy. Gone were the dregs of exhaustion, of pain. What was happening to her? Why? Tears burned her eyes with each footfall. Heavy and sweet, the taste of blood lay on her tongue. Her neck burned, her mind replayed the touch of Gawain's lips against her. The entire night haunted her.

She flexed her fingers, her gaze locked on her hand. Her nails had grown, sharpened like claws. They resembled Gawain's claws. Deadly tools with the ability to cut through layers of flesh. Weapons designed to draw forth blood and kill.

Panic swelled, her heart racing with each

thought dancing through her head. Had she become like him? Was she a killer? A monster set to ravage the mortal world? No, no, it was not possible. She wasn't a killer, a butcher, rather she was a woman...wasn't she?

Gods above, how had it come to this? How had she forgotten what her mother had told her time and again? There were beings out there who could kill with but a touch, a thought—vampire, dragon, demon, all walked the earth seeking the weak. Had she become so weak, so frail she'd fallen into the trap they'd set? If so, how could she get out?

Her stomach heaved, the very idea of leaving Gawain enough to set her teeth on edge. Could she walk away? What would she do if she were given the chance to turn and leave? To leave Gawain, the quest, the life she even now could feel closing in on her?

If given the chance to be mortal, to be what she had been, would her life be different? Indeed, she'd long ago felt the blade of death. Casting a quick look at Gawain, she swallowed against the bitter tide of fear and doubt rising over her. Could she do this?

Perhaps it was more important to know if she could avoid her fate. Would being what she was help save her sister? Could she find those responsible for Una's disappearance as a simple woman? Maybe what happened was an answer to her prayers. A means for her to save Una and herself from the fate the gods had intended.

Aye, it was done and she would accept it. She had to.

"You're a brave woman." The familiar drawl drew her attention to the sky. "You are changing, but you're not becoming a monster, Bede. Remember what I told you, allow him to guard your heart and you will be rewarded."

Taking comfort in the soft whisper, Bede moved a step closer to Gawain, her heart aching at what he must be thinking. Would he accept her? A mortal being within his world?

* * * *

Gawain froze mid-stride for a heartbeat, his body on fire. Dawn was on the horizon, and Bede clung to him. Blood soaked the collar of her dress, and two fang marks stood out on her throat. Her eyes were bright, shifting from side to side, her shiny, partially formed claws digging into his arm as they hurried through the night. The silence between them was tense, filled with questions. How would she handle the truth? Could he break it to her in such a way she'd come to accept what she was becoming with each passing heartbeat?

He sighed and looked at her. Downcast, her eyes revealed nothing, yet he knew she had to feel something. Guilt tickled at the back of his mind. In his own way he'd failed her as much as he'd failed Maudhnait. Selene had given her to him, he was certain, but had his goddess thought of the consequences?

He doubted it.

No mortal wanted to be turned into the being they'd been taught to fear and loath all their lives. Generations of humans had been told the stories of vampires creeping in to steal babes from their beds and drink them dry. Stores of men and women seduced into offering up their necks and bodies to the whims of creatures of the night intent on destroying them.

Swallowing a bitter curse, Gawain squeezed her hand. He would do what he could to ease the crossing, even if he didn't know what exactly he had to do. The thought of doing nothing and losing her enough to make his stomach twist.

Bede was unlike any other woman he had known. Strong. Smart. She would have made an impressive vampire warrioress. There was no frailty to her, no hesitation. For all her faults, Bede was everything a man could want.

King Hemat would stand displeased when he did not return with Una. It was a fact he had accepted. Hemat did not truly understand what he had sent Gawain to do. How could anyone expect him to leave Bede behind and save the child? But then Hemat was a man ruled by his grief, even now centuries later. A king who would never understand the choice he had forced upon Gawain.

"We will find your sister," Gawain promised, wrapping an arm around her shoulders. "I will get you to safety and continue the search."

"Your king wants her. That other thing wanted her. What reason could anyone have for interest in a child? Una is innocent, young." Bede looked up at him, her lips parted, a flash of a fang in the darkness. "If we find her, your king will—"

"No, I think not." Gawain stared into her eyes. Hemat wasn't interested in killing the child. No, his interest was something else, something that was not truly evil - but bore no kindness to it. In Una's sight, Hemat believed he could rid his court of the treacherous and deceitful. Hemat cared nothing for the child, only for what he could gain from her. "Trust me, sweetling. He'll not harm her, he values her far too much for that."

Bede sank her teeth into her lip. A frown marred her face, sorrow in her eyes. Faith was something they both had little enough of, and her doubts were easily read in her eyes. As a mortal she had been abused and sold off like chattel. Now, her sister faced a fate she could not imagine.

The certainty remained, unchallenged by even

fear, Hemat would do, nay could do nothing to harm the child. Selene would punish anyone, even a king, for destroying what she had created, and there was no doubt she'd had a hand in this.

With a sigh, Gawain sought to soothe Bede's fears. "He won't kill without reason. She is said to read the soul, it is fair to assume he wants to have her read those within his court. We are on the brink of a war."

"That is not our..." Bede stopped and stared at him, confusion in her gaze.

"Trust me, Hemat will not risk the wrath of the Great Mother, Selene. She would destroy anyone who would harm a child. Even one such as our king. Selene's wrath is horrific and brutal. Hemat understands she will destroy him and all he touches should he harm the girl."

"And yet Hemat wants Una - that offers little comfort, Gawain. Una is a child. She is alone, with strangers. We both face a future where our death is the only certainty." Bede's voice twisted, a dark note threading through it. "Be it by mortals or your kind - death is all that waits us both."

"No need to concern yourself, Bede. I will protect her."

"And who will protect me?"

"I protect what is *mine*," he snapped, his fangs

flashing. "Any who dare touch what belongs to me will beg for our goddess's touch. Even a king, sweetling. You have my word." He whirled to stalk into the darkness. Raking a hand through his hair, he froze for a second before lifting his hand to his face. The smell of her essence was strong, filling his head as he held his hand before him. A shudder traced over him, the image of her coming apart in his arms flitting through his head. Beauty such as he'd never known, her body arching into his touch, the wash of her orgasm hot on his hand, on his fingers. The very taste soaking into his tongue.

Curse the instinct, the pull. He had no time for a mate, no time to break his vows. Peace only came after the tumultuous and rocky upheaval of war. Blood would stain many worlds before the end - and he could not bear to see Bede among the fallen.

She is your mate, Gawain, and as such she will protect you and serve you. She is a mortal woman, flesh and bone, no more than food. I have never drunk... You drank of her, his conscience whispered.

Bede, innocent and mortal—the mate of a warrior who failed.

Gawain shook his head, his hearing picking up the sound of her footsteps. The wind carried her scent to him, the aroma mixed with his own. Vows or no, he had more to protect than just himself.

* * * *

Tall, lush grass rose up in the clearing. The night air was alive with the scent of heather and fresh water. Silver moonlight cast a shadow across the area, turning every boulder, every nook and cranny, black with shadows.

Walking through the last few trees, Bede glanced around, seeking any sign of life. A look at Gawain shocked her, a faint bluish tint surrounded him, the free-flowing tendrils of their tattoos wrapping around his body. Her eyes focused on the serpent at his throat, the red eyes stared at her with kindness, the fangs retracted.

"Gawain, why is your tattoo so at ease? Its fangs are not..." She waved a hand at his throat, uncertainty prickling along her nerves.

"It's a mating thing." Gawain shifted, the scent of unease filling the air. "Our kind uses them as a means of protection, of identification. We're born with them."

"And mine?" Bede tugged on his arm, pulling him around to face her. Her voice cracked as she touched her throat before dropping her hand. "What of me? I can feel it beneath my skin."

Gawain frowned, tilted her chin up to stare at her throat, an unreadable expression on his face. His fingers traced over the snake beneath her skin.

Bede shivered, the scales rattling together as her beast stirred. Grabbing his hand, she gasped, her body on edge, fire building in her veins. Leaning forward, she pressed against him. "It means we're joined."

"Mated," Gawain whispered, his eyes tracing her features. "Something we cannot have. I would drink you dry during the claiming, Bede. The exchange of blood is important, vital even, to the mating ritual. We need to exchange…and you cannot drink it, you are not yet…"

Bede lifted her chin, the scent of his arousal thick. "I can."

"No, you cannot. I pray she has not let it get so far."

Bede frowned, the faint note of fear in his voice like a plunge into icy waters. What could be the reasoning behind his fear? His hesitancy? Whatever the reason, it wasn't about him drinking her dry. "What would you have us do then, Gawain?"

"Find one of those who knows a gatekeeper. It is rumored there is one not far from here, but it is too far to walk before daybreak. We will seek shelter for the day then approach her."

"That is not the meaning of my question." Bede rolled her lips together. "You can only skirt about the issue so long, my lord."

"I would not speak of it at the moment. Come, we will risk being found if we do not move."

Bede shook her head. Stupid man. His foolish pride blinded him to what was obvious. There was wisdom however, in his words. To stay in one spot was to put themselves in the path of soldiers, outlaws, or worse. "I have heard the steady fall of hooves on the ground. Perhaps it is the horses. We could use them, if we were to catch them."

"We could use them, but the horses you hear are not those we were riding. They belong to mortal men. Come, we must not stay here."

Bede moistened her dry lips, her eyes scanning the area as she nodded. "As you wish, milord. What of the woman you seek? Will she grant you aid? Granted I know little of the ways of these witches but surely she will not turn from your plea."

Gawain paused, throwing her a narrow eyed look. "Take care, Bede. The sorceresses are not eager to help others. Each makes no attempt to hide their demands of payment, and each is often far more costly than it is worth."

Nothing could be more costly than my sister's death. Wisely, she bit back the sharp retort and followed him into the deeper brush.

Shadows spread long, dark along the ground when he stopped and dropped his sword and cloak, then rolled the kinks from his shoulders. Sinking to a boulder, Bede glanced around. The air was thick with the odor of mildew and rotting vegetation. In the distance, she could hear the babble of a stream, the sound of something moving.

"Are you going to hunt?" She eyed the column of his throat, her stomach growling.

"We'll eat when we can. I won't risk it now." Gawain dropped to the ground, wrapped his cloak around himself, and pulled a corner over his face. "Sleep, woman, the walk tonight will be hard. The path is steep, rocky, and will not be welcoming."

Rubbing her throat, Bede curled up on the cool ground, her eyes staring at the sunlight speckling the grass beyond the canopy of the trees. She could feel the heat building already.

"Go to sleep."

Gawain's grumpy command grated on her nerves, but she closed her eyes. Knowing the cantankerous man, he'd make her run the entire way to the witch's house. If he didn't, he'd surely be eager to yell at her. Gods above, the man was going to drive her insane before he secured her sister—or gave in to his lust.

Chapter Twelve

Silver beams of light cast shadows along her sweat-covered skin. Beneath the pale flesh, blue rivers of life flowed. Her breasts rose and fell with each rapid breath, nails scoring his back, his ass. Whimpers of delight filled his head as he bent to bite at the curve between her arm and her breast. Sweet as candy, the taste lay lightly on his tongue.

"Gods above, yes. More, Gawain, more." Bede pulled his head closer to her chest, holding him in place.

He shuddered at the softest of caresses along his cock, her nails trailing through the thick curls around the base. Groaning when she caressed his balls, he lunged forward, pressing his shaft against the softness of her abdomen. The warm evening breeze whispered over the tip of his cock, sending a shiver up his spine as it cooled the moisture clinging to his head.

"Yes." Bede arched up, her thighs tightening around his hips. The hot, wet glide of her pussy against his balls sending shards of pleasure through him with each shift of her hips, each roll of her body.

Intense tingling raced along his spine, settling in the tender sacks beneath his shaft. He could feel the pressure building into an unfamiliar maelstrom. Thrusting forward again and again, he wallowed in her response. In the scent of her that filled his head, and the hot, wet glide of her core against him. "Need to be inside you."

"Now, lover, please, now." Bede whimpered, her nails leaving welts along his back, her teeth at his throat. "I want you inside me, want to feel your seed."

Roaring his pleasure, Gawain rolled his hips, pressing the thick head against her opening. Inch by inch he slid inside. Pleasure rolled over him like the moonlight along his flesh. Rolling his hips, he thrust deeper, his hands pulling her thighs higher, wrapping them around his waist.

"Come for me, Bede. Come around my hard cock. I want to feel you orgasm." His guttural command sent shards of pleasure down his spine. He could feel his scrotum tightening, the pleasure building. With a final thrust he shuddered as her inner walls rippled, tightening, milking his length. He grunted with each spurt of his seed deep within her warm body.

Her body tingled, her core throbbed, a hollow ache settling between her legs. Ragged, her breathing harsh in her ears, Bede wiped a hand across her chest. She stared at the dry, calloused flesh of her hand, her fingers spread.

Gods, it had only been a dream. It was only a dream.

One not of her own. Why would she dream of his dreams? It felt so real. She squirmed on the hard ground, trailing one hand down her body to cup the swollen flesh between her legs. Tiny waves of pleasure that raced from between her legs. Confused, she ran a hand through her tangled hair, her breathing slowing as she calmed herself. "But why dream of his dreams?"

Pushing herself up into a sitting position, Bede scanned their hiding spot. Gawain lay wrapped within the confines of his cloak, his legs spread. Her eyes wide, she licked her lips at the subtle shift of his hand along his shaft.

She stood, weaving slightly on her feet. Bede halted, two steps from him, his grunts of pleasure going straight through to her aching womb. With sudden clarity the truth hit her. She hadn't dreamt his dream—rather she'd felt what he had because they were linked, connected. Mated. The fading confusion settled her racing thoughts.

She was his in every way. Her future was set.

Bede dragged her trembling hand through her hair, pulling on the knots in the long tresses. Beyond the shadows her thin shawl lay in the grass. The pale glow of the sun fell on the worn fabric, teasing her. Without a thought, she strode forward, bending to grab it. Her fingers wrapped around the edge.

Searing agony ripped up her arm. The sweet scent of flesh burning filled her nose. Bubbles spread across her hand and up her wrist, some breaking open to reveal raw, oozing wounds. Jerking her hand back, she gasped, pain ripping into her throat, closing it. Her stomach turned, the meager contents threatening to come up.

Screaming she swayed on her feet. Her eyes widened in horror at the sight of her hand as she pulled it from her chest. Blisters had formed, blood congealed as it bubbled through the delicate flesh. Again and again, her pained cry reached the heavens, her knees giving way as she watched the very skin peel off. Her body was wracked by tremors as she cupped her wrist, the burnt odor wafting up to her nose. The taste lay sour on her tongue.

"Selene! How could this happen?" Gawain's voice reached through the anguish as he cupped her hand. "Bede, darling, what happened? How could so much damage be done so readily?" He lifted her arm, his fingers tugging at the sleeves of her dress to reveal the spreading burns along her flesh.

"I just grabbed my wrap." Bede sobbed, rocking back and forth. Tears burned as they dripped on the wounds. "It…it was there in the grass and…"

"Did you reach for it in the sun?" Gawain's voice shook, his grip tightening on her arm.

* * * *

"Aye, milord. It is my only…" Her voice broke, sobs taking over as she cradled her hand to her chest.

Already the blisters were opening, flesh blackened and smoking, the stench of it burning his nostrils. Pale bone peeked from the sloughing tissue, the blobs of dark, dead blood boiled, the wound the most extreme he'd ever seen. Icy tendrils of fear darted over him as he paused, his mind racing with the realization her flesh had already begun to change, the curse of the sun would lead to injuries so bad death would be the only outcome. Selene's power was more than his simple prayers could allay and it hurt deeply. Her transformation was beyond them, not even a blessing by Selene could change it now. Bede was a vampire, with the weakness of the sun upon her.

"Selene, be merciful!" Gawain pulled her tighter against his chest. His chin rested on her head for a split-second. "Come, we must stop the burning."

"Gods above, Gawain, it hurts. My skin is all but peeling from my bones." She glanced at him, her eyes swimming in tears. He felt his heart stutter at the pink tinge to them as they rolled down her face, leaving trails of the palest color against her white skin.

"Shh, *leannan*, I know. I know. Come." Gawain wrapped her in his cloak, teleporting to the nearest shade closest to a slow-moving stream. Ripping part of her tunica from her, he dipped it into the cool water. Wringing it out, he watched the water drip onto her injury. The hiss of cooling flesh and bone loud in his ears. Her sobs and screams of agony like a brand against his heart. He shuddered at the slow tickle of a single tear running down his face. Tears for her pain, a mark of their union, of their claiming—and he could find no solace in his unanswered prayers.

"It burns, Gawain, it burns. Make it stop." She sobbed, tears streaming down her face.

"Shh, my love, I will," he promised, rising to move behind her. He pulled her tightly against him, his fingers tightening on her jaw. "Sleep, little one, sleep."

His soothing whisper reached through the pain, through the terror, soothing her into a trance. She barely moved, a hitch in her breathing the only indication she felt the touch of his hand along her burnt flesh, a blessing for which he was immensely thankful.

Gawain stared at the injury. He prodded her arm, testing the tissue, the stench of burning flesh sticking to his nose. The wound went bone-deep.

He could see her body trying to repair the damage, but it would take too long. She needed the aid of a healer, one familiar with the mortal body.

Only she wasn't mortal—she hovered between their races until she gained her immortality. Even those born of a vampire union took years to grow into their endless lives.

He glanced at their camp. Sunlight dappled the ground beyond the canopy, the edge of her shawl laying there. Easing her onto the lush grass, he hurried to gather the garment, hissing at the burn of sun on his skin.

Horror ripped through him as he balled her shawl, his gaze landing on her sleeping form. Selene's gifts were expensive, dangerous. Had Selene in her foolishness truly felt he deserved such a woman as Bede? Had Selene saw fit to gift Bede to him in all manner?

With mixed emotions he darted to her and quickly loosened the ties of her attire. Baring the flesh of her chest, he stared at the coiled serpent upon her breasts, it's dark eyes narrowed, mouth closed. Behind it, wings of flame spread across her throat to wrap around her shoulders.

"No! Selene, I beseech thee, take this curse away. I have made vows. I cannot—"

"You can, you must," the wind whispered softly.

"It is your time, Gawain. Embrace your fate and wash away the sins that were not of your own."

"But she is—"

"She will heal if she but sips at your blood. Give her life."

"Or curse her with death. She is mortal, human. Given a choice she would prefer mortality—"

"If you do nothing, she will die. It is you who can choose, and your heart will guide you. You know I speak the truth, Gawain. Give her the blood of your heart and you will be free of the prison from which you hide. You were never meant to do as you have done, vampire."

Gawain pushed her hair from her forehead, his mind fighting what his heart already knew he had to do. His eyes closed, his fangs sharpening, he lifted his forearm to his mouth and ripped into the flesh. Coaxing her mouth open, he watched his life force seep past the plump red of her lips.

She would heal.

He eyed her hand, an icy touch wrapping around him. Muscles, bones, flesh mended slowly, connected until he could recognize her hand. By the rise of the moon she would be healed enough to travel.

* * * *

Curled around herself, Bede watched the flesh of her arm knit itself back together. The itch was unbearable, yet every time she moved to scratch it, Gawain would growl, his dark eyes flashing dangerously.

"Where is this witch? How long until we reach her home?" Bede shifted, her fingers plucking at her tattered clothing.

"We wait for the sun to set." Gawain gestured to the fading sunlight. "Then we will teleport. It will not be easy. They like to hide their places so mortals do not find them. Nothing worse than a nosy mortal wanting to hunt a sorceress, unless it's one who is looking for any immortal being."

"So by midnight we shall be there?" Bede raised her fingers to her lips, her tongue darting out to lick along the still healing flesh. The taste of blood was sweet on her tongue.

Gawain nodded. "Take care, Bede, she will demand payment and what coin I have will be needed to reach my home. Stop that! I'll bind it if I have to." His fierce frown was enough of a warning for her to lower her hand to her side.

Hoping to turn his attention from her picking, she tilted her head. "What of me? Of Una? We are here, we are human. Do you mean to leave us behind to face—"

"You are not human." Gawain rose to pace the confines of the clearing they were hunkered in. "You are blessed by Selene. There will be no going back now."

"Why?" Bede jumped to her feet, her fists planting on her hips. "Why do you fear this so much? What have I done to make you so..."

"It is not you I fear. Gods above, grant me the strength to face this. To save her," he prayed, his voice breaking, pain leaching through the words.

"Do you find me revolting? Or perhaps I am not all that you desire? What is it you seek, milord? I would change it if I could."

Gawain flashed his fangs at her. "I took vows, Bede. I failed. How can I expect to be honored, to be gifted by a woman as pure, as innocent as you if I cannot protect my own queen? If I can fail at such a thing, how do I know I will not fail again? I will not risk becoming less than I am by killing one so precious to me. No, I will not risk you for my failures. In my weakness you will bear the burden of my sins, I cannot—I will not allow that burden to be passed to you. I will beseech Selene to reverse this, to remove your curse and—"

"What of my sister? Do you intend to abandon—"

"Your sister will be found. I am certain the

sorceress we seek will know of her whereabouts." Gawain paced back, his movements stiff as though he were caging his power, his rage.

"And then what?" Bede shook her head. "Then you abandon us both to a fate that is ours? What of my desires? What of my faith in you? Am I so foolish you believe me to be a child?"

"I will see you both safe."

"You have not answered my question, milord. What of my faith in you?"

"Faith cannot undo what could be if I fail to control myself. I will not, I cannot forsake you. I would rather greet the sun than commit such a horrid crime. Don't you understand? I would rather die than risk your safety."

Fury rose, unbidden, as she glared at him. "Then find my sister, sir, so that we may remove ourselves from your presence and be done with this farce. Once that is done, you can slither off to your precious Selene and fuck her."

"I will not bed her. I wouldn't even if I could." Gawain vibrated with his emotions. Anger and passion swirled around them like leaves falling from the trees. "I took a vow of purity. I cannot..."

Bede's eyes widened, and she smirked. "You want to though, don't you? You want to slither into the bed of your beloved little whore. Have her lying beneath you with her thighs spread. Makes sense you want—"

"She is a goddess, *the* goddess. I worship her as the mother of all vampires. As you will if she does not reverse—"

Bede cut him off with an upraised hand. "So be it. The moon is rising. Let us get to this sorceress and be done with it. I would have my sister back with me. Then I shall pray to this goddess of yours to remove this vile curse from me so you can be free of all temptation, or is it disgust? Either makes no difference to me. Only a foolish child would believe the words spouted by the crookedest of tongues, and I am no child." Stalking past Gawain, Bede headed deeper into the brush. Soon she would be rid of the insufferable clod and have her sister with her. If the mere thought brought an ache to her chest, she resolved to ignore it.

Bede's startled shriek pierced the night air when Gawain grabbed her around the waist. Whirling her around, he pressed her against the rough bark of a tree.

"You tempt me, Bede, make me long for things I am forbidden. Do not stir the beast further, I would do right by you and your sister."

"Tempt you? One cannot tempt stone, sir. Do right by my sister and I? Find her and free yourself from your pitiful duty." Bede smiled, an icy twist of her lips. "Then you can return to your vows and wallow. Perhaps you can even bed your whore, or whatever it is you desire to do."

With a strangled curse Gawain jerked her head back, his eyes narrowed, dark slits. "I would have—no, we will finish this later, Bede, my dearest. In due time." Bending his head, he kissed her. His lips heavy, harsh against hers, his thumb pulled her chin down. She shuddered with want at the sweep of his tongue in her mouth.

Tentative, uncertain, she responded. Her tongue darted out to touch his, her hands seeking purchase in his hair. Her fingers tangled in the dark strands as she opened her mouth further. Coercion eased the yearning to punish, falling beneath the need to please. Desire, languid and thick, wrapped through her mind, her body melting beneath his touch.

"We must go," Gawain muttered against her lips.

"Yes." Bede whimpered at the weight of his hand on her breast, her head falling back against the tree. She clung to him, pressing hot kisses across his brow, his nose, his cheeks, before mashing her lips to his.

The feel of his fangs against her tongue was like a caress along her clit. Her leg lifted, wrapping around his thigh as she arched into him. Again and again she moaned at the dancing of their tongues, their bodies saying what they could not. When Gawain pulled back, she stared at him through a haze of want.

"Come." Pulling her against him, Gawain pressed a single kiss to her forehead. "My little temptress. We will finish this, be certain of that."

Bede gasped, her breath locking in her chest at the weightless feel a moment before her feet touched the ground in a small, murky clearing. She could hear the croaking of a frog, hear the crackle of dead branches, and she shuddered.

"Gawain?"

"Shh." He squeezed her hand. "It'll be alright, milady."

"So Selene's favored warrior has shown himself finally?" A low purr slithered from the shadows, drawing a growl from Gawain.

"Amuliana, what a surprise. What cesspool did you slither from today?"

Bede tensed at the barely leashed hostility in Gawain's voice at the appearance of a tall, beautiful blonde lurking in the darkness.

"What's this? Now you're bringing your food with you." The woman laughed softly. "She does not appear to be the babe your king sent you for.

Though I suppose being older, she offers a few benefits a trifle more fun than the babe. Is she enough to tempt you from your vows though? Hmm, more tempting than I? Tsk tsk, Gawain. Such a waste of virility. I suppose I'll need to make do with those who are not so virtuous."

"What do you want?" Gawain pulled Bede closer, his grip tight, painful.

"Simply popping in. Be warned, Gawain of the Ek-leat, Hemat will not be so forgiving if you bring him the wrong female."

"You concern yourself with things of no matter to you. Be gone you disease ridden hag. My king is not so easily seduced by your ilk."

"Perhaps. One need only look to a fallen general to see the truth. Ignore my warning at your own peril." Like her body, her voice faded into the darkness as another figure materialized on the far side of the clearing.

"Gawain, who was that?"

"A petty goddess, one you should guard your back against. She has no redeeming virtues, only the jealous vanity of one of her ilk." Gawain nodded at the floating apparition. "That would be Marshante, she is cursed by Empharo, another sorceress, to be as ugly on the exterior as she is on the inside. To cover the curse, she cast a spell that makes her appear to be a phantom. Powerful, deadly, she is the one we seek."

"Well, well, well…to what do I owe this pleasure?"

Bede gaped at the translucent figure. Shadows darkened under her eyes, her cheeks, and she appeared to have no legs below the knees. Looking into the dark orbs where her eyes were, Bede felt no fear. Instead, she smiled. Boredom, animosity, and a hint of warmth lay within her hollow gaze— in this apparition, she'd found a friend.

Chapter Thirteen

Gawain bowed his head toward the apparition. He shifted his weight from foot to foot, bracing himself as he addressed her. "Marshante, we come seeking your assistance. We seek word on a small—"

"Child, a girl taken from you days ago. And you desire to get home?" Marshante cackled, her pale visage rippling. "I am aware of this. My assistance is not free, however. I do nothing without it being in my favor."

"We have little gold and I must pay the gatekeeper."

"Some other trinket?" Marshante pushed past Gawain and stared at Bede for a moment. She trailed her gaze over Bede from the top of her head to her feet and grinned, revealing blackened teeth and bleeding gums. "This dagger?" A wave of her fingers lifted it from the scabbard to hang before Bede's face. "Rather unique, beautifully crafted."

"Gawain, no, it was my—"

"Mother's." Marshante nodded. "Indeed, I know this. But it is not the dagger I wish to have.

Come, let us sup together and I will tell you my terms for my sight." Tucking the dagger into her bodice, she smiled at Bede before her attention dusted over Gawain, pausing above his heart for the barest of seconds. "Yes, yes, my terms. Come, come, let us sup this evening together, though I fear I cannot offer you the delicacies you are accustomed to. I do not dine upon blood, but perhaps I have a fine wine or something else I can tempt you with."

Gawain glanced at Bede and followed the apparition across the field. They would need to tread carefully, Marshante was benevolent only when it served her. He laced his fingers with Bede's as they approached the small, thatch-roofed cottage. Smoke curled upward, the smell of freshly baked bread strong in the air.

Marshante opened the door and ushered them in with a small smile.

Gawain guided Bede forward, his hand on her lower back. Warmth filled the small cottage from the roaring fire in the hearth. Bundles of herbs hung from the rafters, along with two large leather skins.

"'Tis modest, but keeps me warm and dry." Marshante waved a hand at the rough hewed table and stools. "Sit, sit."

Keeping himself between the two women,

Gawain settled uneasily at the table. "What is it you desire, Marshante? If not the dagger—"

"The dagger is but a tool to get what I want." Marshante puttered around. "Long ago a king, in a fit of rage, cursed an entire people, well several actually, without realizing just how foolish his act was. Innocent or not, he condemned all without a thought, unaware of how desperately he would need those he's shunned. It has taken hundreds of mortal lifetimes to get to this time. Scattered like the four winds, the keys to hold Saltar have all but been lost. Until now."

"What nonsense do you speak?" Gawain tensed, his eyes narrowing.

"I will give you what you seek for a price." Marshante smiled. She laid the dagger on the table, the tip pointing to Bede's heart. "To find the one with double sight, you will need to venture beyond the realm you know. She resides within the temple at Dromberge."

Gawain inhaled sharply. "That is Amuliana's realm. No mortal may enter without—"

"You are not mortal."

"I am not a demi-god!" Gawain roared. "Why would she take the child? What purpose could there possibly be for kidnapping such an innocent girl? Amuliana does nothing without benefit to herself. To steal this child is to bring upon my wrath, sorceress, and I will stop at naught to retrieve her. Do you understand me? There is not a thing which will stop me from retrieving what that whore has stolen from me!" Marshante's eyes flashed dangerously and Gawain paused, leashing his rage. "Forgive me, sorceress, but surely you can see how this child is important to me, to us. I beg of you to grant us any boon you may have so I may right this terrible wrong."

"There are few who can see into the depths of that bitch's motives. Amuliana is an empty vessel, greed and lust have driven any trace of kindness from the god she was meant to be. What I can reveal is the most pressing. She has taken the child to prevent Hemat from knowing the truth. There are threads to the vampire palace, to other beings. I can tell you no more. I do, however, have a warning for you. Beware, there is one who wears two faces and she will betray you all. She is not mortal nor is she vampire. Una will be safe, her fate lives within the heart of a young warrior who you shall cross paths with soon. One of the bound ones who seek a worthy ending to their quest. Condemned for a crime not of his, he wanders, seeking justice. Heed his warning, Gawain, heed it, as it will protect those you care for in this time of unrest. There is more to this than a simple rising of a fallen general."

"Is she safe? I would have her back with me."

Bede clung to Gawain's arm. "Gawain, please. If there—"

"Your fate, Bede, does not follow the path of your sister." Marshante settled at the small table, her visage wavering to reveal a hunched, disfigured crone. Her green eyes narrowed as she stared into Bede's face, her lips curling to reveal crooked, broken teeth. "The fates had grand plans for you and for your sister. In truth, you were never meant to travel the same path. It is rare to have a line with so many branches. Usually only one is gifted, one bears the burden of their ancestry. Yet in you I sense great power, great wealth and love, and in that you share the burdens placed upon you by a grief-stricken king."

"She is but a babe, I must—" Bede grabbed Gawain's hand, her eyes swimming with tears.

"Bede." Marshante paused, her eyes on the dagger next to where Bede clung to Gawain's hand. With a flick of her wrist, she had the dagger in hand and slammed it through their hands.

Bede screamed in agony, tears falling as she gasped. Gawain's roar of fury echoed with her sobs. His fingers scrambled to pull the weapon from their hands. Bede shook as he slid it free, blood pooling between them. He hissed at the smirking sorceress.

"I warned you, my vampire friend, my sight is

not free." She shrugged aside her transgression. "Your paths are united as they have always been, forged in blood and bone. Bound by the same thread. To go home, Gawain, means to understand your war is not over. Guilt has marred you—but it was not your guilt. The one who wears the two faces is responsible for Maudhnait's death."

"Where is the portal?" Gawain clenched his fists on the table. The ache in his hand fading as the flesh and bone mended itself. "You've taken your bounty, now tell me where is the gate I must travel through to reach my realm?"

"Two days hard ride by horse to the north you'll come to a massive wall built by those pesky mortals. The gatekeeper will be near Chesters. Look for her at the setting of the sun. She'll not reveal anything while the Romans are about," Marshante forewarned. "You'll be walking so it will take you longer. Weakened as your mate is, you'll not be able to trace far."

"We'll need to depart immediately. Before the sun rises we should be able—"

"Go at dusk. Let your woman rest."

Gawain glanced at Bede who shivered, her face streaked with tears, sweat, and dirt. She needed to rest, to recover not only from her escape from the sun but from the loss of blood and the feverish pace he'd set.

With a sigh, he nodded. "At dusk. Come, Bede, you can rest here by the fire."

Bede shook her head, her eyes already drifting closed. "Too warm. Hungry, Gawain."

"Rest while I hunt."

"She will be safe here." Marshante put a hand on his shoulder, the weight warm, comforting. "Trust me, for she has awakened within many the beginning of the end. Soon those who have caused all the mayhem will be known to all—and those deserving of their place will be secured."

Gawain bared his teeth. "See that she is safe, witch. Break your word and there will be no place you can hide from me." He strode out into the darkness, the door slamming shut behind him.

* * * *

Bede snuggled deeper into the bedding, her ears straining for a hint of sound to reveal Gawain's presence. She could hear the sounds of the night but nothing more. The whispers of the predators and prey moved in tandem beyond the treeline. The howl of a wolf echoed on the wind. Rolling over, she punched the straw down and sighed.

"You want him." Marshante's slow drawl traced like fingers along her back.

"I hardly think—"

"No need to be shy with me, girl. I have been around longer than you could imagine and have had my share of lovers. Ah once I was so beautiful men lined up to court me." Stepping through the shadows, she settled on the floor beside Bede. The soft whisps of air stirring around her kept her from appearing solid. "He's a vampire. At one point he was one of the king's most trusted warriors. However, he is still a male. The right encouragement and he'll be crawling between your thighs faster than you can hide from the sun."

Bede shot her a dirty look. "What do you care?"

"He wears his scars rather than healing them. Blemishes which are not his to wear. He speaks of a vow, one that is centuries old. It is time he breaks it. He was young and it was something in the old ways. So few of the younger warriors are willing to take such vows, but I think they should. Gawain is fierce, dedicated, a warrior to be proud of. If you want him, there is one thing, he as a vampire, cannot resist."

The bed beneath her groaned when she sat up at Marshante's words. She glanced at the door for a moment before focusing on the phantom before her. "What would that be?"

"He is a man of honor, of integrity, even among his own kind. He is one who does not drink of a female...unless it is his mate. He wants you, wants to sheath himself within your body. If you want him, make yourself irresistible. Has he drunk of you?"

"Yes, we had no other—"

"There are certain pleasure points for vampires." Marshante buffed her nails. "The neck, the wrist...for a mated male the valley between the breasts. Draw him into these spots and you'll have him. If he resists, learn the places on his body that rev him up. I once knew a vampire who got hard whenever I licked behind his ear."

"How would I draw him to those points? He's barely kissed me beyond my lips."

"There is nothing sweeter than the hint of his mate's blood. A tiny prick between the breasts, a drop of blood upon a nipple, all will work. If he's ever touched your pussy, then he would know the scent of your essence. It will work just as well as blood, perhaps even better because it will stir the beast's instincts to mate and you may find yourself with more than you can handle. Though I doubt you'd be displeased with an alpha male betwixt those thighs of yours."

Bede shifted, her face on fire as she listened to the witch's words. Did she want him? Enough to throw caution to the wind and claim him? By the gods, yes, yes she did. He was her man, and she wasn't about to let anyone or anything stand in her way. "I shall learn. He belongs to me, I want him I ache. Yet he always turns away, flees from such intimacy."

"Then take him." Rising to hover above the floor, Marshante slipped into the shadows of the room, vanishing into the flickering flames to leave Bede alone with her thoughts.

Was she willing to risk it all to capture her vampire? Bede shuddered at the thought of Gawain's desire. She could feel the pleasure, the heat when he'd touched her after the bandits' attack. Her body burned at the memory of his hand against her core, his fingers plucking at the hard, sensitive nub at the top of her pussy.

Kicking the covers off, she rose to pace the room. Beyond the door the faint howl of a creature ripped apart the stillness and she shuddered. Trailing a finger down her throat, she paused between her breasts, her eyes drifting shut. What would turn him on? How could she make him shake that control and take her? She lifted her hand, her fingers slipping between her lips, her tongue swirling around it before she drew it along the curves of her flesh, tracing around first one nipple then the other.

Erratic, her harsh breathing filled the room as her hand trailed further down her body to the thick, springy curls between her legs. Tossed about a sea of sensation, she leisurely slid her fingers down to the swollen folds. Her breath caught when she brushed her clit, her body on fire. Whimpering as her fingers slid through the slick, wet heat between her nether lips, she braced a hand on the mantel, her knees trembling.

Taking the few steps back to the bunk, she collapsed, her body undulating with pleasure as she toyed with herself. She dipped a finger inside, shuddering at the tight feeling. Dragging it against her sensitive flesh drew a moan of pleasure. Shivering, she wiggled on the bed, her legs kicking at the tangled blankets.

Lost in the sensations, she barely registered the sound of the door closing. Whimpering Gawain's name, she arched against her hand, seeking something. A muted growl drew her attention a split-second before she felt someone grab her wrist. Her eyes flew open to meet Gawain's dark stare.

"Please." Her legs spread, wrapping around his leather-encased hips. A sharp tug and he fell forward, his hands bracing his weight next to her head. "I need you."

"Gods above, woman, you'd be enough to tempt even the most stalwart man." Growling, he bent his head, his mouth so close she could feel his breath dance across her face. He pressed his lips to her, his tongue tracing over her lips. Sharp teeth tugged on her bottom lip, sucking it into his mouth.

Bede groaned, her hands reaching for him, arms tangled behind his head. Her tongue pushed his tongue out, sneaking into his mouth to clash with his. Hot and slick, their tongues dueled, thrusting passionately. The faint sweetness of blood on his tongue eased the hunger within her only to wake another. Her hips arched, pressing into the hot, hard press of his cock beneath his trews.

"Yes," he hissed, his hands shredding the bed beneath her. He groaned as her fingers pulled at his shirt, baring his chest to her gaze, her mouth. Licking along his chest, she nibbled at the exposed flesh. Her tongue swirled around his nipple, drawing it into a hardened nub.

His groans of pleasure echoed deep within her, stirring the embers of her own lust. Desire coiled within her belly, and she hovered on the edge, her mind flooded with yearning as she wiggled beneath him. The scent of her arousal filled her head, the musky scent of his lust competing to drive her to the brink.

She cried out when he pulled away, his head dipping so he could lick along her throat. He bit at the flesh of her neck, his teeth scratching the surface before his tongue laved the wound. Throwing her head back, she moaned as he trailed kisses down to her breasts, his hands cupping them. Mouth closing over a puckered nipple to lavish it with heated licks, pressing it against the roof of his mouth.

"Gawain, please." Forcing her chest tighter against him, she scrambled to center herself. Heat boiled within her until she was certain she'd explode. Trembling fingers shoved at his trousers, pushing the leather over his hips. Her fingers dug into his ass, one hand sliding around to cup his shaft. He lurched forward, his shaft throbbing in her palm. "Yes, lover. Gods above, yes. I want you. I want to belong to you." She gasped.

Her hips rolled with his, rubbing her aching clit against his shaft. She gasped at the feel of his scrotum slapping against her flesh. His hard cock pressed into her belly, the tip leaking pre-cum with each rolling thrust.

Rough hands shoved her fingers from around his cock. "No, let me." His guttural growl filled her head as he leaned down, his forearms catching her beneath her knees. Sensations flooded her as he moved slowly down her body, his mouth trailing across the bare skin.

A garbled scream filled the room as he licked at the sensitive flesh between her legs. His tongue flicked at the tender bud, sending waves of pleasure slamming over her. Stars burst behind her eyelids, and her fingers dug into the pallet, her body shaking as wave after wave of her orgasm poured over her.

"Now. Oh, please," Bede pleaded, her body aching for more, the desperate need drawing her in. "I want to feel you in me, to feel you..."

"Yes." Gawain pressed a sharp kiss to her thigh, his tongue darting out to lick at the sweat-slicked skin before he moved up her body.

She could feel the hot, hard press of his cock against her abdomen, the thick cords of muscle in his arms pressing against the underside of her knees. Her heart raced, every nerve on fire with each brush of his body against hers. The crisp hair surrounding the base of his dick, the curls dusting his chest, his nipples dragging against her body. She gasped for air, her eyes at half-mast as she stared into his dark gaze. Control had fled, his body and hers rutting toward completion with only the thought of fulfillment in her mind.

Undulating hips, grunts of pleasure, her body on fire, she clung to her lover, her voice strangled as she babbled almost incoherently. Desire flared, dancing, whirling, seducing her into the deepest throes of passion until she sobbed with need.

She felt his hard cock pressing against her stomach, the head moist and swollen. It rubbed against her clit, his hand sneaking between them to guide it. Lost to the sensations of his possession, she whimpered, a lone tear sliding down her face as he slid into her. The pressure was intense, stretching her as he nudged deeper. Tightening her legs, she clung to him as he shook, his hips lurching several times. The hot wash of his seed seared her womb again and again. His roar of pleasure echoed in her ears as she flew apart, her body responding to his pleasure.

Clinging to him, she trailed a lazy finger up and down his back, sweat pooling in her navel as he lay panting against her neck. She tensed when his fist pummeled the pallet next to her, fear pushing aside the remaining tendrils of satiated pleasure.

"Gawain?"

"I have shamed you. I couldn't…"

Bede pressed her lips to his temple. "You pleased me, my love, milord. What more could there be?"

"But I did not penetrate— Gods, I spilled my seed too soon. I couldn't even last long enough to—" He gave a shuddery breath, his head pressed against her shoulder.

Bede wiggled, his softening member slipping from her body. Cool air ghosted over her nether regions, and she pressed kisses along his face. "You did. Rest, Gawain. Rest, for I will want you again and again. This is only the first time, my love. There will be many more of that, I'm certain."

Chapter Fourteen

Curled next to Bede, Gawain traced random lines along her bare shoulder. The scent of sex and woman filled his head. Exhaustion tugged at his mind and body, yet he couldn't rest. The pleasure he'd felt at taking her was unlike anything he'd ever known, and yet he'd disgraced himself.

He'd spent himself before he'd taken her properly. The feel of her hot depths milking the very tip of his length had pushed aside all his control. She deserved to have a more skilled lover. His eyes closed, the sensation of her maidenhead on the head of his cock washing through his memory, he felt himself harden, his length pulsing with pressure. A lifetime of lust burned through his veins, pooling in his testicles.

Longingly, he palmed his hardness, his ardor building. Burying his nose in her hair, he inhaled. His scent mingled with hers, the aroma of sex flowing like water over him. A low growl rumbled through his chest when she stirred, rolling over, her legs falling open as she arched into his touch.

Already he could taste her lust on his tongue, taste her need, and it stirred his own. He hardened until he ached, his body primed for mating. The faint reproach of his vow fading from his mind to be replaced by his throbbing need. There was no dishonor in embracing a mate, taking from the one meant for him. Licking at the pale flesh of her neck, he wallowed in her delicate shudder, in the moans leaving her lips.

"Bede. Oh, Selene, help me."

"Yes." Bede's palm rested on his chest, her nails scoring above his racing heart. "Come with me."

Pushing aside his uncertainty, Gawain bent his head, his lips closing on hers as he thrust his tongue into her mouth. The rising moon would judge him, but for now, he would do what he could to please her, to claim the climax she, nay, *they* deserved.

~*~

Sunlight filtered beneath the front door of the small cabin, drawing Gawain's attention away from the sleeping woman in his arms. The rising sun roused man and beast and he could make out the bleating of sheep. Footsteps on the rocky ground, the crunching of leaves and grass beneath the person's weight. Stylox, he could even smell the scent of sun warmed dirt, but none held the interest of the woman sleeping in his arms.

His woman. His mate. A mortal who....no, he couldn't think of that. Gawain shook his head and pulled her closer. He pressed his lips to Bede's shoulder, his fangs aching. He needed to get to Una, to take her before the king, but what of Marshante's warning of the double-faced one? And what of the king? Was Hemat's intent to use the child then kill her? No mortal had ever set foot within the halls of Dreken—at the very least, none who didn't end up dying.

"Confusing, isn't it?" Marshante appeared by the fireplace. "You want to do as you have been ordered but doubts plague you."

"If I take her sister before my king…" Gawain tugged the cover higher over Bede's shoulder and rolled from the bed, already reaching for his pants. He loathed the idea of being naked before the sorceress. "I will not risk harm to the babe, not when it would mean my chosen one would—nay, I cannot, will not do as I have been ordered if it means death to a child."

"He will not kill the child. Hemat may be many things, but a child killer he is not. No, he knows more of this than he says. He knows her power, just as he knows he needs her too greatly." Marshante settled on a stool, her pale visage drifting like smoke through the air.

"What of my mate? To drag her to our world would mean her end. Hemat may want the babe, but a grown woman? Nay, he'll kill her, and if he does it will leave me empty. I would embrace the sun. Bede needs safety. I have a task. I should leave her..."

"Here? Tsk tsk, warrior, even you must know she cannot remain here. There is danger here you have no idea of. There are humans who would harm her before you could return." Marshante leaned forward. "Even now the wretch who sold her and Una searches for them. Word has gotten back to him of their escape, and those of Luthgor's ilk seek them. He must either retrieve the girls or hand back the gold and he's not want to do it."

Gnashing his teeth together, Gawain stared at Bede's sleeping form. His body ached with a mixture of fury and lust. Turning, he focused on the fury. It was safer, and it fed a ready temper. His mind raced with plans, many discarded like smoke before they'd reached fruition. "I must do something."

"Her safety lies within the realm you must go back to. Here she is mortal, weak, at risk of having her blood spilt by a zealous male. There she would be safe."

"Hemat and his queens will not tolerate her in his court."

"True, but what need have you for his court?" Marshante rose to drift to him. "She is the eldest of the last of the line. A true daughter of Brooxa, of the Ohm Domm. To leave her behind would be to ignore your vows."

"I have forsaken all vows. What sorcery did you use last night, witch? I have spent eight hundred years pure, without worry of the lusts of the flesh, and in one moment, one heartbeat, I forsake those vows." Gawain narrowed his eyes at the cackling woman, uncertainty and embarrassment heating his blood if not his flesh.

"None. It was not I seducing you. Your beast simply rose, responding to the haunting cry of your mate to be possessed. You claimed her, Gawain. You took her blood, knowing you wanted her, knowing she stirred the fires within you, made your cock come to life. Was it as good as I've heard whispered? Was it sweet and rich? More tasteful than your cupped blood? Then the wine you drank so readily?" Marshante cooed. "Did it linger on your tongue, fill your mind with images? Hmm? What, no response for me, vampire?"

Gawain waved a hand in her face, turning with a snarl. It was true. He'd felt a connection, a desire running through him. To drink of her, to take the innocent blood on his tongue, he had done the unthinkable. He spat a curse and whirled to glare at the smirking sorceress. Her words were truer than she could know.

Bede's blood was sweet, thick, rich, it bound them together in a way that none had ever teased him with before. He'd seen the mated, seen those claimed, and watched as his fellow soldiers had drank of their women, seen them fuck them during the celebrations, heard their stories, and it all paled compared to Bede.

He would protect her, even if it meant leaving her. "Perchance, Selene will reverse this curse, and allow her to regain that which was lost." Barely whispered, the words were as false to his ear as they would be to Marshante.

"No." Marshante eased past him. "Her place is by your side. Saltar himself would not change what has come to pass. Selene has blessed you with a fine woman, one of equal power to yours. To refuse it would be to insult your goddess. The gatekeeper will await you two nights hence. Before you reach her, you will meet a young warrior. Hear his words, for he will guide you to what you must do next."

"I need no sunwalker to guide me," Gawain spat.

"Now, why would you assume such a thing? Do you think only those cursed to burn eternally would stand in your path? He is no sunwalker. The man I speak of is a dragon warrior. An outcast and equal to you in many ways. His words you must hear, Gawain, hear and accept." Marshante paused before the door, her body already beginning to evaporate. "Old foes will become new allies, and in their courage you will find what you seek."

Gawain rolled his eyes at the muddled message, his mind drifting to the coming nights. He would need gold, more than they had, to pay for the opening of the gate. He had nothing more than what he carried. Save for her dagger? His eyes fell to it for a moment before he pushed aside the thought. No, he would not betray her by taking that which she held so dear.

"Gawain?" Sleepy, Bede's satisfied voice rose around him.

"The sun is still too high. We go in a few hours. Sleep, Bede, sleep for now."

"I am no longer tired. Where is the sorceress?"

"Gone. She has left us here to seek her penance."

Bede frowned as she pushed her hair from her face. "Penance?"

"Rest, our journey will begin tonight and it will be hard. You'll wish you'd rested."

"I am thirsty." Bede licked her lips, rising from the bed.

Gawain flushed at the sight of her full breasts, her narrow hips, the long scratches of his claws tracing over her pale flesh. Like a wild beast in rut he'd taken her twice, yet she'd not complained. Nay, she'd responded freely, wildly. Soothing any worries he still held over coming too soon during their first mating.

"I'll get you a drink of water."

"Nay." Bede grabbed his arm, her fingers digging into the flesh above his gauntlets. "It is not water I seek." She purred, lifting his hand to her lips. Nuzzling into his palm, she met his eyes. Licking at his thumb, she nudged him until he spread his fingers, her mouth closing over the tender skin between his forefinger and thumb

"She does not have…" Gawain's breath rushed from his lungs. Pleasure raced through his veins with each slow grind of her jaw as her teeth sank deep into his flesh. His eyes rolled back in his head, his knees threatened to buckle. Each slow suck reached through his body to stroke along his hardening cock until it was a physical ache.

"Goddess, you need…"

"Delicious." Bede licked the scarlet liquid from her lips, her eyes heavy-lidded as she appraised him. "So much better than water, milord."

"Damn my soul to Stylox. Woman, you cannot do this." Gawain ground against her, his hand tangling in her hair, his eyes narrowed. Lust raced like wildfire through him. "You are mortal. Do you not realize what you've done?" He spat a curse. No, there was no way she could know. "By drinking of me, you may become ill. Humans are not meant to drink of the flesh."

"Mortals, it seems, are not meant to do much at all. Besides, milord, I think it foolish to call me a mortal human when we both know I am not," Bede whispered against his lips. He could feel the hardened nipples poking against his chest, the sway of her hips as she rolled them against his hard shaft. "Surely I am of some use to you. Do you not want to crawl back into the bedding? Spend a few pleasurable hours before the moon rises?"

"Bede, gods above. Even now, there are those who would hunt me. Who would hunt us both. If I thought for a moment…"

"Who? Who would dare risk your wrath by hunting us?"

"Dragons, Saltar's followers, there are the demon races…those with something to gain would hunt me. Your father even now seeks to find you, so we cannot discount him."

"Father? My father is dead. You must mean — no, why would he. The very idea of his catching me is enough to turn my stomach. I would rather die feeling alive than live without seeking all I can," Bede returned, her eyes flashing wildly. "Do you think I do not see? That I do not know what you are? It is beyond such trivial things. In these crazy times there is naught we can do but cling to that

which is ours. I am yours! In body and soul. To
deny me is to deny you."

"I will not risk your death!" Gawain roared. "I
serve a king who would kill you for but breathing!"

"You breathe. You have always breathed. What
does it matter if I do or not?"

"I did not breathe. It is a trick of my kind. The
hunter must be able to walk among the prey,
Bede. It does not matter now. We will rest, and at
sunset we will head north. We will seek this
gatekeeper and I will find your sister. If it is the last
thing—"

"Una is lost to us for now." Bede pressed her
fingers to his lips. Her eyes swam with tears, pain
locked within their depths. "We must do what we
can to save ourselves. Rest? Nay, I think we will not
rest this day." Bede took his hand, tugging him
back toward the bed. "We are but pawns, milord.
Let us enjoy the peace at least for a few
moments," she whispered, her hand cupping his
shaft and squeezing.

"You would tempt even the stoutest of wills,
Bede. I can barely resist you now, to go further—"

"Gawain, stop protesting." Bede pressed her
lips to his. "You are already lost."

Gawain groaned, his body responding to the
softest touch, to her gentleness. He offered a weak

growled protest when she pushed him back onto the bed, her legs straddling his hips.

He palmed her buttocks, his fingers splayed as she rocked along the hard length of him. Shuddering, he moaned at the pleasure, the melting heat of her core seeping through his pants to moisten his cock. With a rough jerk, he pulled her down, his mouth taking hers in a wild kiss meant to tease. It was truth she spoke.

Chapter Fifteen

A pair of travelers blocked the road Liam was on. The tall male stood in front of a young woman, leashed violence in both their stances. Moonlight played across their faces, the faint red glow from his eyes revealing his nature.

Trapped in a seeming mortal shape he was no match for the vampire standing in his path. Eyes narrowed, malice dripping from his fangs, the Vamp shoved a young woman behind him. Looking up through the branches of a weathered tree, Liam cursed the Fates once again. Liam watched him draw his sword, the blade flashing in the moonlight.

Her long, dark hair fluttered in the breeze, but it was her eyes that held his attention. Dark, wide, they held a secret awareness, a knowledge that reached deep into him. Within the depths something tugged at him, a sense of familiarity. He tensed at the low, furious snarl that shook the night. Instantly, his attention refocused on the main threat.

"Let me pass," he ground out through clenched teeth. He dropped his hand to the hilt of his sword. The cold metal a welcome weight in his palm and he braced his weight. Why had Draconi given him this task? It was better suited to one trained to deal with the bloodsuckers.

"You dare to look upon my woman."

"I looked upon no one, bloodsucker," Liam denied. "Let me pass so I may deliver my missive and return to my hunt."

Liam's attention caught when the woman stepped away from her master. Her steps were quiet, as though not to attract attention. Was she one of those poor fools who willingly lived to serve the vampire? Pity if she were, as pretty as she was. Her plain shift did little to hide her curves or the bloodstains along the neckline. She smiled, a slow, steady shift of her lips to reveal white teeth, and the beginning of an impressive set of fangs.

Liam grunted at the heavy weight of a blow to his midsection. His breath exploded when he hit the ground, his hands catching him before his face hit the ground. His eyes focused on the vampire standing above him, his sword at the ready. He glared at his attacker, and his hand grappled for purchase along the parasite's leg. Catching him behind the knee, he jerked him off his feet and clambered back up. Growling a warning, he could feel his fire growing, the rage pushing against the bonds that kept him in human form.

Teeth lengthened, sharpened, as his fist connected with a solid jaw. Cursing in his native tongue, he pummeled the vampire. His blows deflected. He roared as he soared through the air, landing in a tangled mass of limbs and branches. Jumping to his feet, he pulled his sword, his instinct screaming for him to shed blood.

His head spun as the vampire traced to him, slamming into his temple with the hilt of his sword. Unlike any other vampire he'd battled, this one didn't seem inclined to go for a kill. The vampire fought with claws, with sword and dagger, with his fists, ripping and shredding the flesh along Liam's torso until the air was thick and heavy with the scent of blood. Roaring in pain and fury, Liam renewed his struggles. Catching the vampire around the throat, he threw him at a massive tree, watching it crack down the center as the vampire hit it. The vampire scrambled to his feet and sneered at him.

"So the bloodsucker thinks he can destroy me?"

"I think you're hardly worth the effort, hatchling." Blood splattered across the ground from the cuts on the vampire's lips. "So weak you cannot even transform. Rather pathetic."

Liam swung, his blade kissing the throat of the woman who stood poised, her dagger in her hand. "Your pet is as foolish as you," Liam snarled. "Let me pass and your whore will go free. Try my patience and I'll slit her pretty throat. By the time you get to her, even you won't drink of her blood."

"Nay," the girl panted, her hand outstretched to the vampire. "Gawain, 'tis not—"

"Silence, woman." The vampire lowered his sword. "We shall meet again, dragon. There will be no mercy shown upon our second meeting. That I can promise you. Let her go."

Liam narrowed his eyes, realization slicing into him. "Oh Bollox, you're Gawain, the king's servant?"

"Aye, I am."

"I swear if his lord wasn't so keen to slide into the mother's bed…" He broke off with a growl. Smoke swirled around his head and he straightened only slightly. It was only a fool who dropped their guard when dealing with a vampire hunting. "I am to tell you there is one within Hemat's court who wears two faces, one your king sees and one which will betray you all if given a chance."

"Who is she?"

"I cannot tell you what I do not know. Only that the one who you will seek is close to the king and his queens. They serve him on the surface, but if given a chance would not hesitate to take the throne."

"Do they favor Saltar?"

"I was not informed of such. Who they are loyal to is beyond me." Liam shrugged. "Now, if you please, take your harlot and let me pass." Ignoring the indignant sniff of the tart, he strode past them. The one who called to him, who haunted his sleep lingered in the mortal realm for now. Soon she would be by his side and he wouldn't be alone.

"Wait!" The woman's voice halted him. "Please, tell me if this woman will put my sister at risk. We heard—"

"Only if she is within the court. Beyond the walls of Tarsunilis those who serve will likely be safe. Mark my words, girl, even you are at risk. If the traitor doesn't get you, your master's clan will. They do not tolerate mortal flesh."

* * * *

Bede watched the stranger vanish with a growing sense of unease. Deep within her mind the icy tendrils of fear crept through her mind. Yet it was not her own. Turning, she stared at Gawain who refused to meet her eyes. Reaching out, she touched his arm, only to wince at the fear that ripped through her.

"I do not fear your clan."

"How can I protect your sister and you if I know not who—"

"There is but one way." Bede swallowed, her

eyes burning with unshed tears. "You must not go after Una. Swear to me, Gawain, you'll not seek her out. If this threat is real, it would only end with her demise."

"And what of you?" Gawain demanded. "What shall I say or do to keep you safe? He is quite right, my clan will destroy you. Only a few mortals have ever attended court, and their fate was one of death. The last was drank to death in less than a day."

"I am not mortal, Gawain."

"Nay, my heart, you're something far worse. You're vampire-bred Forsaken. Twice as dangerous to the king, for he will hold you accountable for another's faults. There are warriors who's only purpose in life is to hunt those who show signs of remembering their ancestry, Bede. I would not wish that for you."

"Then we will prepare," Bede snapped, his fear a heady sensation that did little to soothe her. To know it was because of a threat to her - to Una, set her teeth to aching. She would not allow anyone to destroy Gawain - not even a senseless king. "I am not so weak as that, milord. Should they try to kill me, they had best be prepared."

Stalking past him, she ducked beneath a branch. Faint, irritating, the rumble of hunger filled her ears. Was it him? A glance over her shoulder revealed Gawain's scowl, his brows drawn together into a frown. There was no sense of hunger from him, so it was her. Painful, it clawed at her. Swaying on her feet, she leaned against a tree, her eyes closed as she gasped for breath, a hand pressed to her stomach.

"By the gods." Gawain was beside her in a flash, his hand soothing on her shoulders.

"I do not understand, I was…" Bede bent over, her stomach twisting, her body wracked with heaves. Each time she felt Gawain's hand smoothing her hair back, his warmth next to her.

"'Tis the Hunger, Bede. You need to feed but there is no one about. Come, the sun is not set to rise for hours. If we hurry, we can seek shelter and you can feed. I will find what you need."

Bede nodded slowly, her fingers squeezing Gawain's. It had struck so quickly, her body demanding what she needed but was not aware of. Straightening, she met the concern in his eyes. "You wish this had not come to be." It wasn't a question, and she swallowed against the pain in his eyes.

"Aye, if you were not touched by Selene's hand, you would have no need to be seeking to end the Hunger. Nor would you be feeling the pain of the sun's curse. I would rid you of both if it were possible."

Bede nodded, there was nothing more she could say. His regrets were not for her presence, but for the pain she suffered. Like it or not, it was a price she would gladly pay over and over again if it brought her one step closer to the joy she'd come to know in his touch.

"I do not regret, Gawain. I will never regret." Bede pressed a hand to his chest and smiled before curling in on herself as the agony spread through her body.

Chapter Sixteen

Gawain hunkered down, his grip on Bede's arm firm. She licked her lips, her fangs pressing into the delicate skin. An unsuspecting soldier had eased the ache of her hunger, though she couldn't bring herself to feel any guilt. Men had done nothing for her in her mortal life.

Pale silver light lit the area. Isolated, the stone wall rose high into the night sky. She caught the smell of blood, her eyes taking in the flames of the torches, the outline of men pacing along the turrets. Their voices rose on the night wind but remained muffled. It didn't matter.

"What is that?" Bede pointed past the buildings to a small glimmer set against the rocks of a massive wall.

"The gateway. Come, we will need to seek the keeper to gain entrance to my realm. No matter what you hear, do not speak. Those suspected of being mortal have been forbidden to travel through our portals."

"Why?"

Gawain shrugged. "Because Hemat condemned all of Saltar's followers to mortality. He made a deal with those who guard them so any of mortal flesh would perish if they were found near a portal. Come, keep quiet. Do as I say without question."

Bede nodded. Biting her lip, she followed him through the darkness to the stone wall. Curious, she watched him tap the stones, his head tilted slightly.

"Who dares to disturb my rest?" Soft, honeyed, the words filled the air with a warmth and kindness that belied the demand.

"I am Gawain, one of Hemat's warriors. Marshante—"

"Yes, yes, she told me you were coming." The wall wavered and a cloaked figure stepped through. "Told me as well you would be bringing your mate."

"I must get her—"

"'Tis home you wish to go?"

Gawain stared hard at the old crone who eyed Bede like a slab of salt pork. "Open the portal, keeper. King—"

"Hemat will understand naught. You bring one of *his* line into his court and you shall be dealt a blow of death."

"She is *mine*," he ground out, his fingers

tightening on the hilt of his sword. "Any who thinks harm her will feel the sting of my blade."

"Then step through the doorway," she cackled. Her gnarled hands pressed the stone symbols, and the shimmer of water filled the growing dawn.

Gawain reached for Bede's hand. "Come, Bede. You will be safe until I can find the traitor in our midst. If Dorstan comes for us, we will have to fight."

"Gawain, milord, I do not fear what lies beyond the doorway," Bede whispered, her fingers tightening around his. "I fear what lies within your heart. You cannot face an entire army alone."

"I swore I would return your sister—and I shall."

"Not at the expense—"

"Your time to pass grows short."

With a glance at the sky, Bede clung to Gawain's hand as he stepped into the lighted archway. What awaited them? Offering a reverent prayer, she swallowed her fear and followed her mate.

* * * *

Gawain stepped through the light, his stomach twisted in knots. Would his kind accept her? He pushed aside his fear and pulled her with him— into the great throne room of Hemat, King of all

Bloodseekers.

Sitting on the high throne, Hemat stared out over the assembled courtiers, with a bored expression. Lined up on both sides of him, his wives sipped from golden goblets. The eldest of them sat closest to Hemat, a stony expression upon her face.

Gawain cast a quick glance around the room. Two nymphs dancing, their bodies swaying seductively to the sound of Liar. Men and women in their finery clustered around the room, the low hum of conversation broken only by laughter. Beyond the women, several men stood, lust in their eyes. He took note of who of the great army was in court and spat a silent curse when he recognized all but two of his sect.

"You brought the bitch and forsake the one you were sent for." Dorstan's sneer rose above the sounds of merriment.

Pulling Bede against his back, Gawain faced his commander. "I have news on the babe. Rest easy, milord, she will be returned—"

"Kill the mortal!" Dorstan screamed, pointing at Bede. "Kill her now!"

Fury rose like a winter storm, lashing at Gawain's control as the warriors advanced. With a sickening grate of metal against metal, he withdrew his sword. His muscles tensed, fangs sharpened, eyes narrowed at the threat. The hint of blood in the air enough to stir his beast, he plucked at his tunic, the serpent beneath flaring to life. "To get to her, you'll need to go through me. She is *mine*, and no other will touch her."

"Stand aside." Cultured, the roar had men splitting apart, their eyes on Gawain who stood at the ready.

Anger swirled, thickening his blood as he watched his king approach. As tall as he was wide, Hemat had an air of importance, of worth about him that made others look away. His red eyes glowed with emotion, fury, hatred, all lashed into a ball of darkness within his chest. He raised an eyebrow at Gawain's low growl at the flash of a fang in Bede's direction.

"We do not allow mortals within—"

"She is mine." Gawain hissed. "By right, by blood, by Selene's hand! To take her from me, you will have to kill me."

"She is mortal!" Hemat roared. "We do not—"

"I care not what you will or will not permit. She is mine, and she will remain here." Gawain rolled the sword in his hand, gauging the weight, the strength of the blade. He felt Bede's tiny hands against his back, smelt her fear, and it sickened him. With a low hiss he could feel the beast within rising, the slow glide of scales against his flesh, and he knew…his inner demon was waking.

"Milord." The soft gasp of one of the ladies of court drew every eye. She stared, her eyes widened with horror, one scarlet-tipped finger pointing behind Gawain.

He turned, his senses already confirming what he knew. Bede stood, her darkened gaze narrowed, fangs dripping, her throat moving with each breath as her beast stirred, coiled around her neck, its golden eyes glowing, its fangs unfurled. Bede, Forsaken, was once more on the verge of being what she was meant to be.

"Come, surely you would rather have a lady of refinement to warm your bed." Soft, seductive, Hemat's youngest consort swayed across the floor. She smiled seductively, an invitation in her eyes. Her tongue darted out as she drew her nails down Gawain's chest, tangling within the lacing of his tunic. Inch by inch she pulled the leather thongs loose, her free hand trailing down his body to the placket of his trousers. "Surely, milord would—"

"Only if you shall desire to lose the hand," Bede ground out, malice in her voice. Stepping between the woman and Gawain, she reached for the handle of her dagger.

"Enough." Gawain slid an arm around her waist.

He slid his sword into his scabbard. "I'll not hear another word on it. Milord, there are far more important issues at stake than the lifespan or lack thereof of my woman."

"She is mortal," the courtesan whined to Hemat, her lips down turned.

Gawain spared the wench a quick glance before ignoring her petulant behavior. "Sir, you must deal with the issue of the traitor within your court. It was told us by two there is one in your court who wears two faces."

"What nonsense." Hemat snorted. "Dorstan, see that the mortal is roomed below. Gawain, I would speak with you on completing your tasks."

"Harm her…" Gawain grabbed Dorstan's arm. "And all the powers of Selene will not save you from my wrath."

"Dorstan." Hemat's low-pitched warning did little to smooth the disdain from his face.

"Go with him," Gawain whispered to Bede. "I will be along soon." He watched her follow Dorstan from the great hall and vanish into the corridors leading to the private chambers.

When she was out of sight he turned back to face his king. Fury raced like ants along his flesh, his muscles bunched and tight. Primed for battle, he stared, poised to grab his sword if it were needed. The power and poison of his beast flowed through his veins. Any who challenged him would risk more than injury, they risked death itself.

"Gawain, as you are aware, there is a reason we do not allow mortals in our realm. She is food, nothing more. To break your vows and drink—"

"She is mine." Gawain snarled, his hand dropping to his sword. "If I want to drink of her, I will. It is my vow, my honor…"

"Be certain of what you are doing." Hemat strode to the throne and settled back. "Now, you spoke of one who wears two faces. I am no fool, I know of traitors within my ranks. That is why I sent for the babe."

"She has been taken, Anagor stole her. He said she belonged to another. The girl sacrificed herself to save Bede while Anagor nearly killed me." Gawain frowned, a niggling tickle running along his shoulders. Closing his eyes, he focused on where it was coming from, every sense attuned to it.

Sweet, tender, Bede's scent filled his head. She stood before a massive window overlooking the bay and trailed her nails over her skin. Her mind focused on him, her thoughts on the nights spent at Marshante's.

Breaking his focus, he turned his attention back to Hemat who sat, frowning, his red eyes searching the room. It didn't take much for Gawain to assume Hemat was wondering, seeking any sign of the traitor, and he felt a sharp jab of shame.

"I will do all within my power to aid you, my king, but I will not risk my mate or her sister. Selene has blessed me and I will not challenge our mother."

"So be it then." Hemat leaned forward, his lips curling up in a sardonic grin. "Only you would dare to think a mate of your take out food."

"Bede is more than simply food, my king." Gawain exhaled. "She is blessed by Selene herself and in that blessing she will remain."

Chapter Seventeen

"Find the child, Gawain, and return her to me." Hemat waved for a chalice of blood. He stood, his eyes narrowed with unspoken threat. "Ensure the continuation of our world. Do not fail me, my loyal warrior. Find her, secure my crown...and your transgression shall be forgiven."

Gawain shuddered as Hemat transported from the room. Return Una to him. As if he had possessed the child in the first place. Una belonged only to Bede and he would return her sister to her. Heaving a breath, he ignored those who stood gaping at him and stalked down the corridor to his suite within the palace.

Pacing the confines of his chamber, Gawain couldn't shake the weight of guilt. Which transgression did Hemat speak of? The death of their beloved queen or the loss of the child? Failure to deliver the mortal child for Hemat to use? Or perhaps one of the many minor things he had done since Dorstan had gained the king's ear. He couldn't fathom which it could be. Though any of them were grounds for dismissal from his sect, and the binding of his gifts.

With a curse, he debated what he could do

now. There was no giving life to one so long-dead, but there was hope he could retrieve the child. Indeed, he'd lost Una before they'd managed to get her here, risking his kind, the very world he lived in, but it was not the end of things. She was alive, safe, at least until Amuliana decided to rid herself of her.

Pushing past the thoughts of his failure, Gawain focused instead on dealing with his mate. There was no other explanation. No way could she be anything but his. Eight hundred years of temptations had never made him want to break his vows, but a simple touch from her got him harder than a gargoyle in stone. His fellow bloodsuckers believed Bede was something to be reviled, little more than dinner, but to him she was everything.

"So forgiving. Trying to make me believe she doesn't blame me for the loss of her sister, but I know it must weigh on her. If I can return her to Bede, perchance…" He paused. "But to get there would mean going through another portal. I'd need more coin. How to get it without the king knowing? He did want me to retrieve the girl, but he would not allow another portal jump— especially to the heart of Amuliana's territory."

Lighting candles, he moved them to the altar, his gaze lifting to the stone woman for a moment. There had to be a way to reclaim Bede's sister and he didn't intend to allow anyone to stand in his way. If Una was at the temple of Amsuloa, the one place a mortal could attend within Dromberge, there was no way he could take Bede, she'd be at risk by those that worshiped Amuliana. No, he'd have to leave her here, something he could do without concern. Hemat wouldn't dare do anything to Bede, knowing as he did that Gawain would revolt. When claimed, his kind were notoriously fixated.

"I will venture out at moonrise," Gawain vowed, stripping down to his leather trews before kneeling at the foot of the altar. Bowing his head, he focused. "Bless me, Selene, for I seek to return to my mate, my chosen, the one she longs for of her flesh. I ask you to protect Bede and young Una until I can fix the failure resting so heavily upon my soul."

* * * *

Pale light slipped through the sheer, gauze curtains as Bede sat on her bed. The room was opulent. The massive four-poster bed was larger than her bedchamber back home. Ornate tables were covered with pitchers and platters, silver combs, brushes, and several trays of some substance she vaguely recognized as cosmetics. Massive candelabras stood around the room, the candles flickering with light.

"My lady, your bath is drawn." One of the girls hovering in the room called out.

Shedding the worn, stained robes she'd arrived in, Bede sighed and sank deep into the steaming, fragrant water of the bath several women had drawn for her.

"Some things never change," she whispered as two delicate-looking girls bustled around the room. She watched them lay out a pale gown, sandals, and a sheer wrap. They hovered, their voices muted as she washed before rising. Bede jumped when they wrapped her in a large, soft towel and began brushing out her long tresses.

"When will Gawain be here?" Bede caught the gaze of one of the girls.

"He lives in chambers on the other side," the younger of the pair explained. "It is rare for one of his rank to be here, in this hall. It's reserved only for those of the…"

Bede narrowed her eyes, fury rising like a tempest within her. Why would they put her in these rooms when they knew she was his mate? Did they not understand? With each passing second she could feel her emotions swaying, the anger, the disgust, rising until she wanted to rip someone apart.

"Where are these chambers?" she ground out.

"The king's guard is housed two floors above—"

"Oresta, be still. You'll not be rewarded—"

"Leave me." Bede waved at them. "I'll find him myself." She watched the pair scurry from the room, their heads bent together.

Stewing in her anger, Bede tugged the sheer wrap into place. She opened the bedroom door and peeked out. The corridor was cast in shadows. A torch flickered in the silence, but there were no guards in sight. The muted voices of a pair had her pressing her back to the wall as she eased along the darkness. Ignoring the silent guards that stood before two massive, ornately carved doors, Bede darted down another corridor. Her bare feet slapped a rapid rhythm along the stone floor.

Pressed against a door, her heart racing, Bede froze. Desire hit, stirring her blood. Strong, metallic, the familiar scent of Gawain's blood filled her head. Her breasts felt heavy, and heat pooled between her legs as she opened the door a crack.

Kneeling before a carved stone altar, Gawain rested on his heels, his head bowed. Bede glanced behind her before stepping into the room and closing the door with a soft click. She shoved the deadbolt into place and stepped deeper into the room.

"I do not wish to be—"

"Milord." Bede paused, her breath catching in her throat. "I..."

"Bede." Gawain stood, his jaw dropping.

Bede offered a small smile, her fingers unwrapping her cloak to let it pool in a shimmering heap at her feet. Heat flared in her body at the lust in his gaze as it traced over her naked curves. Her fingers trailed up her throat, pausing at her lips. Tracing the outline of her lips, she dipped a finger into her mouth, sucking on the digit gently before pulling it out.

She shivered as his eyes followed her movement as she trailed her fingers down her throat. Her nails followed a silent path down her body, stopping to tease before she dipped them between her breasts, up to the puckered nipple. Twisting it between her forefinger and thumb, she couldn't help her ragged breathing.

Bede watched his gaze follow her touch. From her nipples to her abdomen. She caught the faint hitch in his breathing when she slid her fingers through the curls at the apex of her thighs. Gasping when she brushed over her clit, Bede shuddered at the wave of electricity rushing through her. Swollen and throbbing, her folds yielded to her touch, and she whimpered at the moist heat.

"Gods above, Gawain. I yearn for you and they wanted to keep us apart," Bede whispered. "I want to feel your hard cock within me, feel you fill me until I don't know where you stop and I start."

"Bede, precious." Gawain strode through the darkness to grab her. Scorching, his lips pressed to hers in a passionate kiss. His tongue stroked along hers, the rich taste of him strong in her mouth.

She whimpered at the feel of his palm on her breast. He rubbed the aching tip, his hips pressed against hers. Her hips rolled, rubbing along the hardened length behind the smooth leather. Desire rose like a raging river, flooding her mind and body.

"Oh!" Bede clung to him when he lifted her against his hard chest. She shuddered as he sat her on the edge of the altar. Icy stone did little to cool the heat flowing through her. "Gawain, what?"

"Shh." Gawain growled, pressing a biting kiss to her jaw.

She shivered as he trailed a hand roughly down her body, palming her heat. Hissing in a breath, she writhed when he slid a single finger into her. He pumped it in and out, pushing her closer and closer to the edge. Her head slammed into the wall behind them, her fingers reaching for his shoulders as he bent his head to bite and suck at her nipples.

"Yes, come for me," he bit out, his fingers moving quicker and quicker until she felt wound tighter than ever before.

She moaned when he dropped to his knees, his

palms smoothing down her torso to her hips before spreading her thighs. Hot, smooth, the flesh of his shoulders brushed against the tender skin of her inner thighs. Bede closed her eyes at the first glide of his tongue against her clit. Arching into the sweep of his tongue, Bede clasped her thighs around his head, her voice squeaking out with each brush of his lips against her core. A strangled scream escaped when he slid his finger into her depths, his tongue flicking at the swollen nubbin at the top of her folds.

Her orgasm swelled, pushing at the boundaries of her control as he thrust his fingers into her again and again. Her thighs tightened, her heels digging into his back. Bede swallowed a scream of frustration as he pulled back, his arms swinging under her knees, forcing them back until she was spread for him.

"Please…" Bede stared into his eyes as he stood, a fine sheen of sweat on his chest.

"My pants." His growled command brooked no argument. Without thought, she ripped the lacings free and pushed the material over his hips, swallowing at the sight of his hard cock glistening with pre-cum.

Her toes curled as he pushed her legs higher, spreading her open completely. She gasped when he leaned forward, his dick sliding into her hot, wet sheath. His hips rolled forward, thrusting against her again and again. Each slow glide rasped against her flesh.

Frustration built, her fangs lengthening as she grabbed his head. Mashing her lips to his, she forced her tongue into his mouth, sweeping it along the inside until he groaned. Her fingers tangled in his hair, nails scratching the flesh until the succulent scent of his blood filled the air.

"Yes, yes." Mindless, her chant echoed between them as his thrusts increased in speed and depth. Beneath her ass, the cold, hard altar shook, statues and candles falling off as he rocked into her.

Grunts and groans filled the room. Random mutters slipped past swollen lips. Bede nipped at his throat, drawing blood. Her tongue lapped at it for a second before she tipped her head back, screaming as her orgasm ripped through her. Gawain's grunts filtered through the haze, and she arched her hips as he pounded into her. The first jerk of his cock within her revealed his own orgasm. She clung to him, tears of pleasure racing down her cheeks.

The crash of the chamber door drew both their attention. The haze of her orgasm faded into a wave of pure rage as she caught sight of three armed warriors, their eyes narrowed on them.

"Milord, Gawain…"

"Out!" Gawain roared, his fangs sharpening, dripping with venom. He grabbed the bedcover tossed across a chair nearby, draping it over her as he turned to confront the intruders. "Now!"

"We heard…"

Bede gasped as Gawain launched across the room, his body primed for battle. Snatching at the falling bed covering, she wrapped it around her, fury and embarrassment laced tightly in her blood as she stood and paced behind Gawain.

"How dare you enter my chamber when I am with my mate? I should rip your throats out."

"Begging your pardon, we heard something break," one of the guards stuttered, sheathing his sword. "We meant no disrespect to your mate." The trio backed out, their gazes not on Gawain's furious figure but on Bede hovering behind him.

Chest heaving, Gawain turned to face Bede who stared at the door. Would he cast her out now that she'd been discovered in his room? Was it forbidden to be—

Her thoughts were interrupted by the low purr coming from him as he strode toward her. With a grin on his handsome face, Gawain lifted her against him and hurried to the bed.

Bede moaned in pleasure when he collapsed on top of her, his hands already stripping the blanket away, his lips on her throat. Wrapping her arms around him, she wallowed in the sensation of his skin on hers, the scent of sex, sweat, and power hanging in the air.

Chapter Eighteen

Bede sighed, her eyes fluttering open. Absently, she reached for Gawain, her heart faltering when she encountered cold sheets. She bolted upright in bed, her eyes scanning the room. Broken candles littered the floor, a tangled mass of fabric flowed over steps to pool at the base of the altar. An intricate metal rack hung from the wall, bare of any weapons.

Swallowing against the rising tide of fear, Bede kicked the covers off and paced across the room, the cold floor seeping into the soles of her feet. Where had Gawain gone? Was he still here within the confines of the palace? Why had he risen from their bed? Her mind raced amid the growing uncertainty that he'd left her.

"Milady?" Hesitant, a young girl hovered by the door, her pale eyes darting between the rumpled bed and Bede.

"What are you doing here?"

"Lord Gawain has asked that I show you to his home. He does not feel you should remain in the palace." The girl fidgeted, her eyes lowered.

"Why? Where is Lord Gawain?"

"I do not know. He did leave you a note, if you can perchance read. He instructed me to read it if you were unable." She pulled a thin slip of parchment from the front apron of her shift, her hand outstretched. "He would have left it here in this chamber but he feared another may come to wake you before I could arrive."

Bede waved a hand at the girl, impatience rushing through her. If Gawain was serving his king, why had he not woken her? Unless Hemat had summoned him to punish him. Should the king feel the need to do so, she would remind him of his duty. Gawain was loyal to the king - and it was time the king acknowledged and appreciated that fact.

Clearing her throat, the servant unfolded the note and began. "Bede, it is best if you follow young Ashalia, she will guide you to the safety of my home. None will dare trespass within the confines of my walls. I will join you soon, but first I must honor my word to you. Una will be safe."

"Ashalia?" Bede frowned.

"Yes, mistress."

"How far is it to my lord's home?"

"Beyond the walls of the city."

"Then I gather I shall need some attire to journey there?" Bede glanced down at her naked flesh.

Ashalia smiled and shrugged. "Lord Gawain has ordered you several beautiful gowns. They should be at his home by now."

"I need something to wear before then."

"Oh, I'll transport you. Lord Gawain instructed me to serve you until his return."

"When will that be?"

Ashalia shrugged indifferently and bent to pick up the sheer wrap Bede had worn the night before. "If you are uncomfortable, wrap this around yourself. We will go as soon as you are ready."

Bede took the wrap, pulled it tight around her form, and sighed. She'd have a word with Gawain when she saw him again for certain. Tensing when the girl grabbed her hand, Bede gasped when the room shifted, splintering into fragments before they vanished. Several heartbeats later, she swayed, her eyes taking in the simple stone walls of a much smaller, simpler room. A small fireplace laid dormant, logs piled neatly beside it. Rough-hewn timbers had been put together to form a rickety table. In the corner a huge rope and straw bed sprawled out.

Hanging from the rafters of the cabin, several leather pouches swayed back and forth. Inhaling, Bede's eyes widened. Wine! The bags were filled with wine.

"Do you hunger?" Ashalia reached for a glass, her eyes on the bags.

Bede shook her head slowly. The hunger she'd felt wasn't nearly as strong as she'd thought. "Not as yet."

"Lord Gawain did say if you hunger there would be provisions. I believe he spoke to Lacet, one of our healers."

"Thank you, Ashalia, but it's not a concern at the moment. I'd like to dress." She gasped when Ashalia darted across the room to lift the lid on a trunk. The speed with which the girl moved was overwhelming, although not unbelievable. As the girl rummaged in the trunk, Bede appraised the room, inching toward the window. "Tell me, does the sun rise here?"

"Yes, but thankfully it does not stay high for long. A few hours at most."

"Good." Bede sighed. "I'm rested. Come, let us tidy the house while we wait for Lord Gawain's return." Work was always a welcomed distraction.

Bede lifted a simple gray gown and slid it on. She stood impatiently, eyeing the thick layer of dust that covered the room, while Ashalia laced the gown up before pulling her long hair back and tying it with a ribbon

* * * *

"Let me pass, gatekeeper." Gawain tightened his grip around his sword hilt. "I am bidden to do my king's business and do not have the time to delay."

"Your heart is not with your king," the slim, treeish figure declared. "If it were, you'd not be so inclined to disobey the rules."

"I must pass. There is a task I must complete."

"She is beyond your grasp." He waved a hand to reveal the glowing symbols. "Still, your heart is pure. I will grant you passage...under one condition."

"Name it and it shall be yours."

The gatekeeper leaned forward, the smell of earth on his breath. "Assume nothing. Beyond this gate there lies a world of mystery. Beware one who would interrupt your quest, enemy of old he may be, he is also a threat to the future. When you return, see that you bring me the sand with which you step upon."

"What need do you have for sand?" Gawain wondered aloud.

"None, to pass you will agree to my terms."

"Done," Gawain swore, his gaze steady on the

keeper.

"Pass."

The shimmering light flickered and danced, allowing Gawain to pass through. He shuddered at the caress of magic along his flesh before he stepped out into the warm darkness of a world unseen to him before.

Stars filled the sky above him. The winking lights flanked the full moon's brilliance. In the distance, he could see several massive structures. Their pointed roofs lifting to the sky, hundreds of torches light corridors and pathways disappearing and reappearing between the structures like veins. The scent of mortals wafted along the night air.

Striding past a massive stone statue, Gawain studied the lay of the land. His eyes narrowed when they caught on two human figures in the shadow of a colossal triangular building. He neared them, every sense vigilant. Tension radiated, his body on high alert at the faint odor he couldn't recognize beyond the fact that it belonged to those of the underworld. It seemed unlikely a demon would expose himself to the mortal world, but one never knew.

"Well, well, what has the gods dropped into our lap but a bloodsucker." His horns flared, eyes narrowed, the larger of the two males eyed him with disdain.

"Indeed, how trite."

"No more than your presence." Gawain braced his feet apart, his hand on his sword. "What is it you seek?"

"Naught," the smaller of the two drawled. "Save to avoid your pathetic war. 'Tis rumored your kind has betrayed your own laws and crawled back into bed with the dragons. One would think you'd kill your enemy less they rise from the grave. We have no desire to be part of your war, or to give homage to the foul criminal you protect."

Gawain shuddered, fear rising like bile to scald the back of his throat. Had Saltar risen? He had not heard of any break, but his mind had been consumed with Bede. Hoping to change the direction of the discussion, he glanced about and asked, "You know the area?"

"Why would you assume we would think to aid you?"

"Demon, try me not. It will not end well for you," Gawain snarled, his teeth gnashing together. He would not back down from their slight, nor yield to a challenge.

"What is it you seek?"

"The Temple of Amsuloa." Gawain eyed the pinking horizon in the distance. "There is one within it I must retrieve." Nerves frayed, he watched the pair share a glance. He needed to get the child, needed her to be whole and safe to ease the worry of his mate.

"You seek Amuliana? She is as twisted as knotted rope. Still, we understand you worship her. Isn't one of your own imprisoned because he was fool enough to take to her bed?"

"'Tis not the lying bitch I seek, but a child she stole from us. I must retrieve—"

"Make haste then. If she stole a child—she'll not return her. Probably dined upon her innards."

"If she has—" Gawain's fangs sharpened, his claws aching. "It will be the last sup she takes. I swear it upon the head of my king."

"Make haste. The sun rises. Seek shelter amid the temples and shafts of the mortal's constructions. Armosi, the city where the temple stands, is two days hence east. No man may enter so I pray you've brought a female to aid you."

"What reward do you demand?" Gawain reached into the front of his tunic, his fingers tightening on the limited wealth he carried.

The larger of the demons laughed, a boisterous sound that startled nearby birds into a flutter of wings and squawks. "You amuse me, vampire. You quest for a child, no wealth, no glory, what more could we ask for but to continue our amusement at your expense."

"My mate and I thank you." Gawain bowed, his attention on locating shelter from the sun.

"Mate?" The pair shared an uneasy glance. "Your mate?"

"Aye." Gawain nodded quickly. "The babe belongs to my mate. The gods will smile upon you for your aid this night." Gawain gathered himself, tracing away from the two stunned demons into the cool, stone cavern of a tomb.

Chapter Nineteen

Flickering light played across the floor, the crackle of wood and flames filled the air. On every shelf and mantel candles burned, oozing wax along their columns. Muted sounds trickled over the air like water.

Blankets lay strewn about, tangled on the floor with the pale glimmer of a gown. A long-forgotten cloak the only cover on the bed. Taut skin covered the delicious curves of her hips, her breasts. Beneath the pale flesh tiny, blue rivers raced, pulsing through her with unfettered life. Restless, her body on edge, Bede tossed about in Gawain's bed. Her hair was matted with sweat, her face pale, gaunt. Full lips parted, moist, begging to be kissed, to be nipped at. Lush breasts rose and fell, cupped in her soft hands, her fingers plucking and tweaking the nipples into hardness.

Scarlet nails dragged down alabaster skin to tangle in the curls at the apex of her thighs. She slid her glistening fingers along the swollen, moist folds of her sex. Hips undulated, rolling with each slow insertion of her fingers into her depths.

Moans of need flowed over them, desire a ruthless master. Each slow movement a torment, building, twisting the need within him until he could feel her agony as she hovered above the abyss. Yet no matter how she moved, how she caressed herself, he realized with cold clarity she could not step into the flames beckoning her so arduously. Aching, tears of palest pink flowed down her cheeks to soak the bedding beneath her.

"Gawain! Gods, I need..." Bede's tormented cry filled the air, her hand moving faster and faster as she fucked herself with her fingers. Biting at her wrist, she whimpered at the slow drip of blood oozing over her skin to fall on a beaded nipple. Each splatter spread a path across her skin leading to her heart. Her fingers trailed through it, painting a faint, hazy image of his brand upon her skin.

Blood stained the tips of her nails as she writhed in agony. Her fingers plucked at her nipples, teasing them. Whimpers of dismay, of pain, filled the room. He groaned at the misery upon his mate, the lust strong. Brutal, unforgiving, the master of her body, of her lust, played her much as one would a harpsichord.

Gawain groaned in searing pain, the vision floating behind his closed eyes. He could feel the icy trail of a tear down his face as he leaned against the wall. It echoed the aching in his groin. Soon, he would return to her. He would give her all she craved.

Chapter Twenty

Silence stretched in the early evening air as Bede lay tangled in bedding. Tiny footsteps darted about the room, and Bede cursed Ashalia's presence. The girl barely allowed her to move before seeking to please. Frankly, after seven turns of the moon, she was sick of it. Nerves were stretched to the breaking point, and if she heard her name in *that* tone one more time she was going to snap.

Snuggling deeper into the bed, she breathed deeply. Flames of longing curled around her. Her body ached with need, with desire for Gawain. The softest of materials abraded her skin. Coupled with the servant's irritating presence, Bede was ready to kill.

"Milady, shall I fetch you something to eat?" Ashalia hovered at the foot of the bed, her hands folded before her.

Bede grimaced, the very thought of food repugnant. Nay, she craved something else. Something to lay sweet upon her tongue, sustenance she could sink her teeth into. For a split-second she eyed the girl's pale throat before shaking off the thought, it would not taste nearly as sweet as her mate.

"Nay, crave no food. Just wish to sleep,

Ashalia." Bede closed her eyes, mayhap she would sleep and dream of Gawain's return.

"Here." Ashalia touched her shoulder. "Sip of this. Milord left it for you."

Opening her eyes, Bede swallowed the urge to throw the girl aside. "Ashalia, please, just leave me be."

Ashalia leaned closer, holding the cup out a little closer to Bede. Her nostrils flared at the familiar scent. Bolting upright, she grabbed the simple wooden cup, her eyes wide as she licked her lips. Taking a sip, she moaned in pleasure. The heady flavor of it easing one hunger as it slid warm and sweet down her throat. The taste lingered on her tongue, teasing her taste buds.

"Did Gawain leave more?"

"Yes, milady. There is enough to enjoy several cups a day for a complete moon cycle."

"Excellent." Bede clung to the cup, her lips pressed against the side. She could feel her fangs lengthening, sharpening to points. The rumble of her stomach eased with each sip.

Ashalia smiled and retreated, her steps silent. A moment later, a gold gown lay over the foot of the massive bed, a matching cloak atop it. Bede fingered it, smiling at the softness that caressed her fingertips. Still, she didn't set her cup down.

She sipped at the nectar within it, her mind swimming in a haze of pleasure as her hunger eased.

Her knuckles white with her grip on the cup, Bede allowed Ashalia to dress her. She hissed at the girl when she reach for it. A soft, sad smile on Ashalia's face was like a blow to her heart and Bede offered a weak smile. "I'm sorry."

"There is no need to apologize, mistress. You miss your husband." The young girl's smile at the task so filled with joy she couldn't find it within herself to halt the process. Dressed and ready to start her day, Bede pushed aside the second hunger, the one building steadily within her mind and body. Each shift of the fabric against her breasts only heightened her arousal until she was ready to scream. She settled at the table and watched Ashalia bustle about the small home.

Her body started at the sensations darting over her. Unseen fingers trailing across her throat, lips pressing at her breasts, calloused fingers on the sensitive flesh of her inner thighs. She jumped at the brush against her clit, her legs opening of their own accord. Desire flowed like wine along her body, pooling between her legs, her sex moist, throbbing.

Wallowing in the sensations, Bede screamed at the crash of the front door as it flew inward, smashing to bits against the wall. Ashalia darted to her side, her hand clutching a dagger, her eyes narrowed. Fear swirled, soaking the air around Bede. She put a hand on Ashalia's shoulder, the other already reaching for the dagger she'd strapped to her thigh.

"It would be best if you didn't." Guttural, the snarled command drew her attention to the tall, dark warrior standing in the doorway flanked by four others. All wore leather covering their torsos, their bare arms marked with swirling designs. None were empty-handed.

"How dare you enter Lord Gawain's home? You are forbidden…" Ashalia stepped in front of Bede.

"Be still, girl." The leader waved her aside. "It is not you we seek. By order of the king himself, Gawain's harlot is to be returned to the palace to face him."

Bede narrowed her eyes, fury swarming over the lingering lust. "You dare to challenge Gawain? To challenge me?"

"Challenge you?" He snorted. "What challenge? You are but a disposable food source. Pity Gawain's decision to break from feeding on females is with one so weak."

Bede shuddered at the banked lust in the man's gaze, his eyes lingering on her breasts. Stepping back, her eyes darted to the others who stared at her much like a slab of salt pork. Her fangs ached, lengthening with the perceived threat, but fear kept her immobile. She screamed when one threw Ashalia aside, the girl's body crumpling against the stone of the fireplace. Rushing past the male, she knelt next to the girl, her fingers seeking any sign of injury.

"Gods above, how could you? She is but a child!" Bede glared at the offending warrior. "You are no better than the Roman dogs who have ravaged my country for so long. Hardly worthy of the title of men. When Gawain hears of this you will suffer."

"Silence, woman." He grabbed her hair, lifting her to her feet. He pulled her flush against his body, and she gagged at the feel of his erection pressing into her back. She snapped at his fingers with her teeth when he groped her breast.

"Selordan, enough. The king has commanded we return with her. He said nothing about breeding with a mortal."

"Pity." Selordan sniffed at her hair, his erection jumping beneath the leather of his pants. "Still, he will grant us permission after he passes judgment. I relish the idea of sampling the blood flowing through its veins."

Striking out, she clawed at his face, his neck, tears forming in her eyes as she struggled against his grasp. Sobbing when the air around them shifted, tightened, she barely registered the long, jagged scratches marring his flesh, or the lengthening, the sharpening of her nails into claws. Her screams and struggles faded from the cabin a moment after she did.

Hard stone met her knees as her captor dropped her to the floor of the mighty throne room. Scrambling to her feet, she glared at the men, fury lashing at her control. Eyeing the nearest man's waist, she smirked when he backed up, his hand falling to his sword.

"You're a traitor," Bede ground out. "Less than—"

"My king." Selordan bowed as the air shrank and a moment later Hemat sat atop his throne. "As you ordered."

"So Gawain thought he could remove you from my—"

Hot, merciless, her blood boiling, Bede faced the king. A low rumbling growl escaped her throat as she eyed the fat blob upon the throne. "Save the bluster." Bede sniffed disdainfully. "We both know you've decided to sentence me for some crime you dreamed up. I am not guilty of anything and yet you fear me. So order my death, sentence me to some dreadful end. You will not get the revenge you seek. Get it over with, and I can assure you, Gawain will avenge my death."

"Be still your tongue, mortal, before I cut it from your pretty face." Hemat leaned forward, a glimpse of his fangs flashing, as if to intimidate her.

Bede shook her head. Did they all think her a weak, frail thing? Had none learned anything? She was no mortal, nor a lamb among wolves. She was Gawain's mate - his chosen. And she would not bow to any of them. "Why? Do you think I must make my own death easy upon you? Nay, I'll not be the willing, whimpering frail mortal you crave. You'll get no obedience or submission from me. Leech." Bede caught the muted gasp of those in the room, but refused to look away from their king.

Hemat's face was red, blotched with fury as he rose to his feet. His boots thudded against the steps as he paced toward her. She shivered at the malice in his gaze, her fingers tangling within the folds of her gown. If she could get it high enough, she could retrieve her weapon. Clawing at his wrist as he grabbed her throat, she narrowed her eyes.

"Tell me, mortal. Are you like all others? Weak, so frail a slight tightening will suffocate you?"

"I am not weak," Bede gasped, her nails scoring his flesh. "Nor do I fear death. But you do." She dropped her voice, a thread of mockery weaving through it. "You hate Gawain so much for failing your queen. But where were you? What were you doing when she was killed? Wallowing in the pleasure between another's thighs, be what you were doing? She was your mate, your other half, and you were off leaving a young warrior to stand guard while your trusted general walked unimpeded through the halls. Oh no, the failure is upon our head, it gnaws and scratches at your wretched. Gawain carries a burden he should not. If anyone should wear the crown of guilt, it should be you. Kill me, Hemat, King of all Vampires—but it will not return what is beyond your reach."

"Kill the bitch." Hemat dropped her, searing pain washing over her as her knees came into contact with the stone. "Gawain should know better."

"Be still your weapons!" Harsh, the unyielding feminine command shattered the tension.

Bede turned her head, studying the figure rapidly approaching from the massive doors. Tall, delicate-looking, her long, dark hair streaked by white, the woman stopped mid-room with her arms crossed beneath her breasts. The woman's eyes scanned the room, disdain and fury sparking in them. Behind her stood two women dressed in leather, weapons hanging from their hips, braced for battle. Fangs and claws at the ready, their bodies alive with what looked like birds on fire.

"Bruja, this does not concern—"

"It concerns us all, Hemat. How dare you kill this child, she has not even grown into her instincts. Newly claimed and you seek to kill—"

"She is mortal! Mortals are no more than food, they serve—"

Behind the woman a familiar figure shifted, her gown wrinkled, blood staining the bodice. Bede gnashed her teeth and turned to throw the men who had kidnapped her a hard glare.

"Ashalia, take Bede to my suite. See that she is bathed and dressed accordingly."

"My queen." Ashalia limped forward, her body bruised, her eyes downcast. Ashalia leaned down and helped Bede to her feet. "Apologies, mistress. I was unable to attend you sooner."

"Ashalia, the fault lies with others, not you. That you came at all is appreciated. It is I who must apologise and thank you." Bede whispered as she shuffled toward the queen. "Your Majesty, I seek only to be returned—"

"Do not fear, child." Bruja cupped her jaw tenderly. She brushed her thumb over the tender skin along her jaw and tutted. "Ashalia tells me you have a dagger."

Bede glanced at the young girl before nodding. "It belonged to Mother. While I am grateful for your assistance—"

"I do not wish to take it. I simply wish to see it." Bruja held out her hand, her long, scarlet and black nails sparkling in the light. "I had a dream, my dear, and I would know if the dream was simply a dream or as I suspect a vision."

Uncertain, Bede gathered the hem of her gown and reached for the dagger. She pulled it from its sheath and held it up. The ornate handle fit her palm perfectly. The stones in the handle winked and danced in the firelight, turning the blade a multi-hued shade of blue. Bede offered it to the queen with a shaky hand.

"Marshante has told me of a gift." Bruja spoke calmly. "Of unlocking a key meant to save our people from the treachery ruling this court. She spoke highly of such a gift. Spoke very highly indeed." She squeezed Bede's hand around the hilt before she pushed Bede's fist and the dagger to Bede's chest. "Go now, child. Rest after you are bathed. My warrioress will protect you." Bruja cast a look around the room, fury and something much darker in her gaze. "I give you my word. It will be as I have commanded. Any who dares to challenge will suffer my wrath."

"You risk much, wife." Hemat's voice was thick with warning, his eyes glowing and narrowed.

"No more than you, husband." Bruja stepped past Bede, her fingers tangling in the collar of Bede's gown. With a swift downward motion, she ripped the back out of Bede's gown.

A startled scream escaped Bede's throat as she scrambled to gather the ruined gown around her nakedness. Whirling, she stared in horrified shock at Bruja who offered a faint smile. Beneath her skin, a familiar warmth began to spread. Embers, stoked, flames licked at her body. Her skin crawling, the soft click of scales rustling filled her ears. Bede clenched her fists, her claws digging into her palms. How dare they! Every muscle coiled, Bede shifted her weight to the balls of her feet. Damn then all if they thought—

"Oh my, Selene, forgive me." Selordan dropped to his knees, his head bowed. He trembled slightly, his palms pressed to the floor in supplication. "I do not beg for mercy for there can be none. I have committed a grievous act."

"What evil is this?" Hemat leapt to his feet, his pale face almost translucent. "She wears the mark of—"

"Bede is the daughter of none other than Brooxa, descendent of Kalli."

"She is of the ilk Saltar..."

"Do not make such a judgement again, husband. Only a fool would make the same mistake twice." Bruja gestured to those gathered. "You sentenced innocents to their demise in a fit of grief. Letting your rage and your loss guide your hand in a foul act you will never be able to atone for. You did it and forgot those who served my beloved sister also served me, served the other queens. You dare to threaten to kill one of my warrioresses! You say she is mortal, husband…" Bruja stepped closer, her gown dragging across the floor. "Tell me then, how is it she seeks not mortal food but rather sups upon blood? How is it she burns at the light of the sun? Do you believe you are more powerful, more knowing than Selene herself! Mother of all vampires, goddess of all!"

Hemat glared at her, his fangs lengthening, dripping as he stepped forward. "You challenge me? It would do you well to remember, Bruja, you are only my consort. Your place at my side can be given to another."

"Then replace me, Hemat. It will not be an easy task. I doubt there are any of my sisters eager to take the position when they are all aware of your loyalties. Ashalia, see that Bede is bathed, fed, and dressed as a woman of this court. Feliara, seek out a sorceress, I have need to speak to one." Bruja glanced around before smirking at her husband. "I do so hope you'll enjoy your days, milord. My sisters and I have closed our chambers to you. Reinstate Gawain—return him to his mate—and we may forgive this transgression. Deny us this, and all the wrath of Selene will haunt your days and nights!" Bruja whirled, her gown fluttering behind her as she stormed past Bede and out the door. Her guards nodded to Bede and Ashalia before escorting them into the corridor.

Bede hurried along behind them, her grasp on her attire desperate, a niggling sensation pulling at the back of her mind. Her heart dropped with fear when two doors swung inward and Ashalia ushered her inside.

A massive tub sat full of steaming water, the scent of roses strong in the air. Several girls stood holding torches and feathers. Long curtains hung from the ceiling. Beyond them, she caught the flare of light off something. Stepping to the side, she gasped. Armor hung off a statue. Gold and silver links raced along the top of it. Two sword hilts rose above, curving to reflect golden wings.

"Beautiful, isn't it?" Ashalia whispered.

"Indeed. Does the queen wear…"

"Goodness, no." Ashalia smiled. "'Tis your armor."

"Mine? I am no warrior. I only wish to be with my lord, Gawain."

"You shall be." Ashalia nudged her toward the tub. "But you must take your place within us again. Come, let me assist you. Once bathed you'll feel ever so much better."

"I doubt it will be so" Bede shed her ruined gown and slipped into the hot bath, her dagger clutched to her chest. "I shall feel better when my mate is home." She sighed, the faint sound of a door closing barely penetrated the growing fog in her mind.

"He will be soon." Bruja patted her shoulder. "Before his return, I think it is only fair that you understand the full truth."

"Your Majesty." Bede scrambled to get out of the tub. Only to halt when Bruja pushed gently on her shoulder and shook her head.

"You are one of us. Of our kind. Forsaken centuries ago. Many centuries ago we were at war with the dragons. There were those among our ranks who used that war to their own end. Saltar was one of them. He wanted the throne - and Mundhait as his queen. She refused him. He killed her for it. Now, there are whispers among those who guard his prison that he seeks freedom."

"Saltar. Yes, I heard of him. Gawain does not think he is free." Bede raised a hand to touch her throat, her fingers dragging across the raised flesh that coiled beneath the surface. A serpent of fire.

"He is not. He can never be free, Bede. Because he will rise a plague upon our land and upon all who stand against him. It would have been more merciful to kill him, but Hemat wasn't prepared to be merciful. In his wrath he condemned Saltar to eternal imprisonment. You are part of a very special group, Bede." Bruja hunkered down by the tub, her gaze steady. "You are a gift to us. Part of a line that was broken. One that holds more power then even Hemat has. Your line is directly descended from the fourth daughter of our Goddess, Selene. You are a member of the Ker Tai-Ak clan, and a gatekeeper in your own right. Within you lies more power than you realize. Together, with others like you, this war shall pass quickly and victory shall be within our grasp. 'Tis not an easy thing, my dear, but you shall be stronger for it."

"You misunderstand. It is not that I doubt what you say." Bede inhaled a deep breath. She looked away, her mind racing. IT was all too much, too fantastic to be believed. Yet there was truth within the queen's words. "My loyalty is not to your king. My loyalty is to my husband and my sister. I may be coming into my gifts as you say, but I will never be a servant to a man who would kill simple because he sees one as mortal."

"Your loyalty to Gawain is powerful, but his loyalty—"

"Is to me. Do you so readily forget he was willing to challenge your husband for me? Gawain is more a man than Hemat. I do not swear featly to you or to any other." Bede leaned back in the bath. "So take heed, queen of vampires. If I must fight I will. But it is not for your king. It is for my husband and my sister."

Bruja chuckled and nodded. "Dreken will burn if Hemat does not open his eyes to the strength and the power of those he has shunned. Aye, you are a true daughter of Dreken. I will call Gawain home to you. Bath, rest. If you have need of anything, anything at all, Bede, demand it." Bruja declared, bustling from the room, followed by two armed women.

Bede stared after her, unease, uncertainty, and hope tangling within her chest.

Chapter Twenty-One

Massive stone pillars stretched into the night sky. Fire roared in cauldrons at the entrance of the temple. Men, women, mingled in the courtyard. Singing in an unfamiliar language drifted to him on the wind. A low, rumbling growl filled Gawain's throat so close to the harlot's temple. So close to Una. He lifted his gaze to the sky and tracked the sliver of moon. Time was running out. The dawn would come soon, already the horizon was turning a pale blue.

Pain flared in his arm and he lifted his sleeve. A dark, purplish bruise discolored the flesh in the form of fingerprints. He did not need to look to know there were similar marks around his neck. he had felt her pain, felt her fear. Their connection was strong - stronger than any he had ever heard of before. Yet now, there was nothing. An emptiness that yawned in front of him worse than anything he had ever known. He couldn't sense her, couldn't feel her. It was as if someone had severed their connection.

Perhaps Selene had granted her a boon. Maybe she'd been given her life back. He snorted, Bede wouldn't turn from what she was becoming. Despite his prayers and his hopes, he knew it was not possible. Bede was his. Turning his attention from the wound, he focused on the throng below. A familiar figure stepped into the moonlight, his pale flesh and hair standing out. Gaunt eyes stared vacantly at the mortals who had come to pray, and Gawain's lips tilted at the corner. Indeed, he would have much fun with this.

Sliding the long blade from its sheath, he teleported to the shadows at the edge of the courtyard. Anagor's presence told him he was spot on. Una was here, and he would return her to Bede no matter who got in his way.

Rancid, and rotting, the stench of disease and death clung to the sunwalker's skeleton-like figure. Gawain's nose wrinkled in distaste.

Anagor grimaced, revealing his fangs had shrunk beneath his gums. He had to be starving, and endless, agonizing demise no-one would be able to speed along.

"I did not believe you would let it be." Anagor shuffled toward him. The older vampire swayed on his feet. Eyes vacant, he stared out over the courtyard. "A man of honor in these troubling times is such a rarity. Most are willing to sell their souls for a bit of coin. But not you. Ye would walk through fire, face an angry goddess, anything to ease the ache of a lost child."

"I will have the child or your head." Gawain

grasped his sword. "I made a vow and I will honor it."

"A vow? To whom?" Anagor turned to him, gaunt face twisted into a darkened mask. Threads of black criss-crossed his face. His lips were thin, chapped. There was no sign of the strength of their kind. In truth, he looked like a horror story told to scare children. Gawain stepped back. He choked back the rising burn of bile.

"Nay, you may take my head, but it will not be my end. Death is not my companion, you see, Gawain. You have come seeking the girl child, but you are too late." Anagor shook his head and leaned against a stone statue. "The fates have other plans for us, Gawain. You, of all of of us, should know this."

"If you have killed..."

"Nay." For the first time since Gawain had met him, he appeared resigned to more than his fate. "Selene has blessed the child and it is her kindness which will keep Una alive. The girl is young, and will grow into a beauty, of that you can be certain. However, she has no memory of her sister, Amuliana saw to it. For Una, her life is focused solely on the service of the goddess which watches over her. You will not find her here. Or on any plane you seek. If you wish to find her, look to the future, Gawain. Una's fate, her future, lies within the arms of the warrior who you've met. Young

Liam is Una's savior in time. Until then, Una must remain under Amuliana's care for the moment—so she can be safe."

"Why would you think I would believe anything of a male who drank his own mate to death while she carried his spawn?" Gawain ground out. "Aye, you took to the field of battle afterward as if what you had done was no more consequence than putting upon your boots. A woman, a child, you swore to protect with all of your being - killed by your own hand."

"Yes, yes, I committed that crime. I have paid for it endlessly for three hundred years. I near my ninth century in this world and every day I beg the mother for death. For the ability to join my beloved in paradise. It is upon my shoulders, I carry such a burden. I would ask you, though. Will you risk the girl child's death?" Anagor glanced behind him, his brows drawn together. "Amuliana will rise shortly. If she looks upon you, Una's life will be in danger. I have no desire to take the child's life, but if Amuliana orders it, I will have no choice."

Gawain hesitated. Anagor's words rang true. He was a slave to his mistress, mindless, her orders were to be followed without question. Still, to leave... "How can I trust you will not slaughter her anyway?"

"You cannot. You must take it on faith, Gawain." Anagor stepped closer, his voice dropping to the barest of a whisper.

"Gawain, you must not endanger the child. Seek her another time." Queen Bruja's voice filtered through his head like smoke. *"Quickly, you must return to us. Bede is in danger."*

Rage filled him, his body tensing, fingers tightening on the hilt of his sword. He turned from Anagor, his eyes narrowing. Who would dare to challenge him? Hemat would not dare to go against their laws. Attacking the *claimed* mate of another, especially one of such power as he had, would mean death to the fool dumb enough to go after his mate. Even a king would not be beyond the wrath of an enraged vampire looking to defend his other half.

"Go," Anagor wheezed, pulled by an invisible hand toward the temple doors. "Return to your world before all is lost. I will do what I can, if it be the only thing I do. My tarnished soul will protect the child as much as possible."

Gawain waved aside Anagor's fading voice and teleported to the chamber he'd spent the day in. His instincts fed his rage, sending flames shooting through his veins. His fangs ached, splitting his gums until the tips dragged against the flesh of his bottom lip. Clenching his hands, Gawain snarled at the bite of his claws into his palms. He roared, a challenge to any who dared to touch his mate. No matter who it was, they would feel his wrath, he vowed. They would all perish by his hand if they harmed his Bede. It was more than the instinct, more than just the mating of two vampires, fate had thrown them together. Gawain froze, realization dawning. Bede was his by fate, by a choice of a god, but he loved her by his own choice.

"*My queen?*" Gawain hoped she would hear, hoped Bede would survive long enough for him to return. "*Please, protect her until I can get to her.*"

A portal formed, opening into a shimmering pool of blue. Sucking in a breath, Gawain stepped into the light. Every sense alert, his heart pounding in his chest he inhaled a desperate breath. The faintest of scents of his mate and the heady scent of fresh blood and anger greet him.

* * * *

Bruja stared at the sleeping woman on her lady in waiting's bed. Dark mahogany hair spilled in waves across the pillow, the tattoos dancing beneath her skin. Proud, strong. Bede was no wilting flower. She was vampire bred, reborn into her own lineage and yet she did not bend to the whims of another. Her loyalty was not to a crown or a king. No, Bede was everything her line had once been and what they could be again.

To gain her trust and her loyalty would take time, effort. Things Hemat would not see come to pass. His rage burned even now. He focused it solely on an innocent woman, blinding himself to what lay beyond the walls of the palace.

An army gathered, their great force clustered at the edge of the forest. All with but one thought in mind. They came for the girl, for her head. With her death, Saltar would feel secure in his plans. With Bede's death, Saltar would not hesitate to make a move to free himself. The coward didn't know the woman he hunted - or the strength she held.

Gawain had chosen well.

Turning, she moved to stare out the window, her gaze following the horizon. Saltar's loyal soldiers waited. Their lord's will like a worm within their black hearts. She could clearly see the flares of fires, of torches, as they assembled, plotting their attack. Weakened by the distance from her mate, Bede would stand no chance against those killers. Yet, she would be forced to fight. Freshly blooded, mortal, immortal, vampire or ally of the vampires, it would matter naught.

"Majesty?" Ashalia approached carefully. Armor encased her figure. A sword hung from her hip, a bow strapped across her back, the quiver full of arrows.

"Soon, child. Has my husband thought on his actions?"

"Indeed. He wishes to speak with you, and summons you to the throne room."

"For all he is, Hema is a good man." Bruja smiled. "Tell him I will see him here in my chamber. Tell him the army is growing, I can taste the darkness within their souls."

"But he summons—"

"In my chambers, Ashalia. Quickly now."

"As you wish, majesty."

"Ashalia, return immediately. You will need to assist Bede in her preparations."

"She is strong enough?"

"No." Bruja listened to her servant's fading footsteps. With a sigh, she voiced her fears, praying silently she was wrong. "No, she is not. Her power comes from her love with Gawain, from the purity of that love. Until he comes, she will be weakened."

Chapter Twenty-Two

Roused from bed, Bede stared at Ashalia as she laid out a simple, yellow shift on the bed. Leather pads and laces. Gloves. With each item laid out, her stomach dropped a little further. Bede cleared her throat.

"Ashalia?"

"Yes, mistress?"

"What are you doing? I feel as though there is something I'm missing."

Ashalia paused, her hand hovering a leather gauntlet. She straightened and faced Bede. "I was commanded to prepare you, mistress. We are at war and soon the enemy will be at our door. Queen Bruja insists you are dressed for the battle."

"I am not a warrior. Up until very recently I was a farm girl who spent her time in the fields. How does she think I am to fight when I have no training? No skill."

"You had the skill to defeat your enemies and get her." Ashalia licked her lips and shifted from foot to foot. "It was a command so we cannot disobey."

"You will find, I do not do well with commands. I am not bound by anything or anyone in this court.

My loyalty—"

"It is not a matter of who is in court, Bede," Ashalia explained. "They come for you. If they get to you, they will kill you and any who stand with you. You are a vampire, and perhaps you have not had decades of training, but you are far stronger than anyone here. My grandmother used to tell us stories of the women in the Ker Tai-Ak. Fierce, strong, warriors to put any man to shame. If you will not fight for the king - then fight for your husband."

Bede exhaled a trembling breath. "We will do what we must, Ashalia. Gawain would not hesitate to protect me. I must do the same for him. Help me dress so that we may face this enemy."

Ashalia smiled and lifted the shift. She dropped it over Bede's head and guided her arms into the sleeves. "You will put them all to shame, mistress. I know it."

Bede doubted the young woman's words, but held her tongue. She stood, lifting an arm, a foot, moving as directed while Ashalia dressed her in the armor and secured her dagger to her side along with the two swords at her back.

Ashalia held out the helmet and stepped back. She gave a quick jerk of her chin and gestured Bede past her. Together, they walked in silence down the corridor and entered the main hall.

Feeling like a painted doll, Bede stood next to Ashalia. Lined up around them were hundreds of warriors hovered. Expressionless, she could only guess they waited for Hemat. Unease flared, no good could come of putting her in armor.

Bede leaned over to whisper in Ashalia's ear. "What is this about?"

"We are at war." Ashalia offered a sad smile, her gaze darting to those assembled.

"War?" Every muscle tensed, her eyes darted to the harried-looking man striding into the room, his body covered by heavy, gold armor. A chill raced down her spine as he turned to face those assembled.

"It is a sad day when we are threatened by the filth that has tainted our kind for centuries. In two days hence, our red moon celebration will be upon us. Tonight, however, a blood moon shall rise. Saltar's army has stirred, rumors of his return have given life to their hopes. We must fight yet again to protect our kind. Blood shall be spilled, lives and limbs lost, but know no fear, my warriors. We shall have victory."

"What of the mortal?" A voice rose above the murmurs. "Who will guard her?"

"Guard me?" Pulling her dagger free, Bede pointed it at the upstart. "Guard yourself. I have not survived Roman legionnaires, slavers, and your kind to need you to hold my hand."

"She is no mortal." Bruja waved aside the warrior's concerns. "My warrioress will fight with you this day, Bede. Death will come for some of us, but we must do all we can."

"My wife is correct. We are at war—let us focus on battle, not on one's weakness," Hemat commanded. "Dorstan, you'll protect the left flank. Take two of your captains and set up a parameter. Selordan, take a legion and escort the women and children to safety. Send them into the caverns beneath Mount Transulvia. They will be safe there. Leave enough men to guard them securely."

"As you wish, my king." Selordan bowed low before striding from the room, his men following without question.

"King! They've breached the western wall. They'll be upon us in seconds."

The tormented screech of a wounded soldier sent a wave of fear through the room. Bede stared at the young vampire as he fell over, a battle axe sticking from his back. Every ounce of her nerve quivered. Was she strong enough for this?

"They've arrived!" The warning came seconds before the first wave teleported into the room. Steel clashed with a mighty roar filling the room as men and women rushed to the fray.

Whirling, Bede ducked the blow of a pale-eyed vampire, his blackened fangs dripping. Lunging forward, she sunk her dagger deep into his flesh, twisting it before jumping back.

Slashing, cutting, Bede hurried through the mangled bodies in the room. Hot, pulsing blood splattered across her face. Anguished screams ripped through her ears, shredding any innocence left. Terrified, she stared into the disfigured face of a vampire man. He was missing a couple of teeth, his eyes dark, void of anything beyond hate and rage. The flickering of the torches lit the bloody sword as he lifted it above his head.

Without thought, Bede grabbed his throat, her hand burning. Searing agony washed up her arm a moment before he started to scream. Blue flames licked up his body, his flesh began to boil and blister. Dropping the weapon, he reached for her wrist, his eyes begging, pleading for an end.

"Death comes to those who are deserving." Bede dropped him, spinning her armor and deflecting the blow from a sword.

Screaming in pain, Bede grappled with the warrior pulling her hair back, exposing her throat. She could see his fangs sharpening, the hollowness of them as he leaned in. Sinking her dagger deep into his neck, she used the force of a kick to pull it from his flesh. Stumbling back, she whirled, her dagger poised, to nod at Ashalia who tossed a sword her way.

Catching it, Bede snarled at the warriors pressing in on her. With a battle cry on her lips, she charged, sword swinging, slicing through flesh and bone. Blinking to clear her eyes of the scalding blood that splattered her, Bede rallied what little strength she had. Ducking, she slid the blade between the ribs of one warrior drinking of the king's guards. The young vampire girl slid to the floor. Bede stared at the blood oozing from the woman's neck wound through two narrow holes.

Bede whirled around, her eyes widening at the massive fist that swung toward her. A startled scream echoed through her head at the agony blossoming on her face. The blow lifted her from her feet, sending her careening across the room to slam into the wall. Sliding down it, she felt a bolt of pure emotion race through her, Gawain stood before her, his eyes locked on hers before darkness claimed her.

Chapter Twenty-Three

He stepped into a nightmare.

Blood splattered the walls of the throne room. Bodies littered the floor. Screams of agony and rage filled the air. Through the battle, Gawain spotted Bede fighting with a larger man. His heart in his throat, he started toward her. A roar escaped as she crumpled to the ground, still, lifeless. Gawain tossed aside any who got in his way as he raced across the room to where she was lying. Please, please, please. The soundless prayer clung to his tongue.

Loosening the armor that covered her torso, he cupped her face. The warm stickiness on his fingers drew his rage like poison from a wound. Pulling his fingers back, he stared at her blood streaking them.

"Bede, beloved?" Leaning forward, he shifted her, untangling her until she was lying flat. "Selene, be merciful." He pushed her hair back from her face before standing.

He reach out, closing his hand around the enemy's throat. The warrior lashed out at him, claws ripping through the air in front of Gawain's face. Soft tissue gave way beneath his claws, hot blood poured over his fingers. Gawain met the warrior's gaze, the fury and hatred in the man's eyes searing into his memory. A cursory glance revealed a bedraggled black bird carved upon the man's chest. Inhaling, he caught the stench of fear, the bloodlust on his enemy, and growled, a deep, animalistic sound. Fangs dripping with malice, he pulled the warrior to him and grabbed the man's jaw. Pushing upward the other man's head on the floor and threw his body aside. He stormed through the crowd, shoving allies out of his way, and ripping into enemies, his red vision locked on his prey. His roar of grief and fury rose above the clash of weapons.

"Wretched bag of bones." Gawain embraced his rage, his desire to kill, throwing yet another man across the room. He withdrew his sword as the vampire crashed through the throne and landed in a broken, bloody heap on the floor.

Swinging his blade, he sliced through two, tromping over them as he made for the scent clinging to his nose. The one who had struck her would die, would burn in the sun and beg for mercy before he gave him what he craved.

Fangs sharpened by anger ripped at the necks of those fool enough to try to stop him. Each blow, each strike from an opponent only inflamed his need to slaughter, to punish. Gawain braced his feet, his body primed as three of them raced at him, their curved swords raised high, their eyes narrowed in fury and disgust. Whirling, his left foot swung up, kicking the legs out from under one man. As he fell, Gawain swung his sword up, slicing his head from his shoulders. The others barely paid their companion a thought, striking at him with claws and fangs, their weapons lost in the melee.

Grabbing the one on the left, he wrapped his hands around his head, snapping the neck as easily as twig. Before he could regenerate, Gawain sliced his throat, dropping him to the floor. The third grabbed his hair, pulling his head back, baring his teeth to drink only to scream in agony as Gawain drove a slim, bejeweled dagger into his throat. He jerked back, shedding his coat, his weapons, every ounce the warrior.

~*~

Bede groaned, agony pounded in her head, her jaw felt as though it had been split in two. She lifted her hand, hands tightened around her shoulders, dragging her across the smooth, cold floor. Forcing her eyes open, she stared up at Selordan. He eyed her with an unreadable expression. Tensing, she reached for the dagger she carried.

"Be this what you seek?" He held it out to her, hilt first.

"Thank you." Bede took it, clutching it to her chest. Struggling into a sitting position, she glanced around. Two massive columns protected the chamber, beyond it though she could see the battle. The floor ran with rivers of blood. Men and women lay in tangled heaps, moans and screams of agony and pain clashing with the sound of swords, of axes and maces colliding.

Her eyes connected with a figure on the battlefield. His back bare, bloody, she could see the scales of the snake wrapping around his torso. The lines of its body coiling around him as he warred with three vampires, his fury displayed to all. Several of them had fled from his reach.

"Gawain, I must…" She winced as she struggled to her feet.

"You must rest." Selordan put a hand on her shoulder. "Daughter of the Moon."

Bede turned to face him. "What did you call me?"

"Daughter of the Moon," Selordan replied. "Your ancestry is descended from Selene, goddess of life. Favored, if you will."

"I am hardly…" Bede pushed herself to her feet. Fanciful and demented, that seemed to be the mark of all Gawain's kind. "I have no time for this. My man is out there…"

"Aye, your mate, my master."

"Gawain is no one's master."

"For my sins against you, I must attone. My life or death is his."

"I've no time for this. Move out of my way."

"What will you do when you get out there? Kill them all? Do you know who is friend and who is foe?"

"Only those who dared to touch him." Bede pushed past him, her gaze locked on Gawain's impressive body. Power flowed through her body, seeping through each pore until she felt invincible.

"Take care." Selordan offered a sword. A frown marred his face when she shook her head and pushed it aside. "There are those out there with no willingness to forgive."

Bede laughed, a cold, cruel sound. "I'm one of them." Stepping from the shadows, she deflected the blow from a half-rotted specter hanging on despite the blood flowing over his face and down his throat.

Sliding her dagger's blade into his throat, she moved through the crowd, her attention on Gawain's figure. Whirling at the heavy weight of a hand on her shoulder, Bede swung outward, the blade slicing through flesh. The warrior's features contorted, swelling, burning as he screamed, clawing at his face. Those around her froze, staring in horror as smoke curled upward from his frame.

Flames soon followed, licking along his body, swirling around his form until he dropped to his knees. The stench of burning flesh filled the room as he incinerated and faded into a smoking heap of ash.

"Bede." Gawain's roar drew her attention.

Ignoring the way Hema's warriors moved from her path, she eyed the invaders. Hissing and snapping at her, they backed away, running headlong into death as she stepped through them. Pausing next to Gawain, she turned, her fingers light on the hilt of her dagger, the weapon hanging from one hand.

"Kill her!" The screamed order echoed above the confused melee.

Bede gasped as Gawain's nails dug into her hip, pressing her back tight to his. She sucked in a deep breath at the burning which started at her throat and radiated out. She grabbed hold of his hand, her nails digging into his flesh as she pressed closer. Through a haze of gold, she watched the invaders advance.

Ruthless, brutal, the bloody battle moved in on them. They crowded them onto the balcony with a single-minded determination. Death would part her from Gawain if she did nothing. Gods above he would risk all for her and be ripped from her arms again. Swords flashing, Bede felt Gawain tense.

With a quick shake of her head, she cursed the fates. There was no way in this world or the next she would let him do whatever it was he was planning. If he ran, he'd regret it, no matter if it were to protect her.

"You can do this, Bede. Reach inside, touch the power of the flame. Cast out the evil in this house and cleanse it." Soft, pure, the familiar voice filled her head. *"Prepare it for the return of your sister, and for the birth of your future."*

"She's burning!" Ashalia's terrified voice swirled around Bede, who stared past her to the amassed army. There would be no peace until they'd departed. The rolling, searing wash of heat flared, catching the invaders in burning clusters. Screams of torment and agony filled the air before they vanished in a cloud of smoke and ash.

Looking down, Bede stared at her hands. Flames licked along the fingers, blue and gold hues dancing from her to the enemy pressing in on her from all sides. Shock ripped through her as she realized just who Ashalia had been screaming for.

"Gods above!" Bede whimpered, her gaze flying up to meet Gawain's. Glancing down, she stared at the fading flames, her fingertips trembling. "What? I don't, Gawain, help."

"Bede, my precious, precious Bede." Gawain pulled her close, his fingers tangling in her hair.

"Gods, I …"

"Gawain! What manner of creature did you bring into our folds?" Hemat's roar shook the rafters.

Bede tensed, her fingers tightening on her dagger, eyes locked on the king who strode through the crowd toward them. A chill crept through her blood, what would his penalty be? Would her act cost her a future with Gawain? Her trembling hand found Gawain's, returning the gentle squeeze.

"Well? What do you say for yourself?"

"Does it matter?" Gawain stepped forward, his bare chest glistening with sweat, dried blood cracking with each movement of his body. "She risks much to save your throne."

"Nay," Hema denied, his gaze a heavy weight on Bede's chest. "She risked it for you. Her instinct woke and she was willing to risk death itself to reach you."

"She is mine."

Bede hid her delighted smile at Gawain's impassioned declaration, even as she stared Hemat down. It wasn't about risks but about what she was. Would the king accept her or cast her out? She couldn't stop the shudder of dismay at the very notion until she felt the slow curl of

Gawain's hand.

"Hemat, husband. Do you risk the wrath of Selene over something so small?"

"She is from that line, and I will not have it within—"

"Grief makes a mockery of you." As hard as steel, a new voice rose from the shadows.

Bede's eyes widened as a familiar figure strode forward. Her long, dark hair was pulled back with a gold comb. Flowing robes of gold and silver covered her ample curves. Blue eyes assessed the room before landing on Bede. Overwhelmed, she bowed her head. This woman held more power than she'd ever known.

"Goddess, you surely do not expect—"

"I expect you to respect my wisdom, Hemat. King of the Vampires. Lord of the undead, master of the night—yet mired by your own grief in a world of hatred and intolerance. It was this very sin which has cost you so greatly."

"Selene, she is..." Hemat shifted beneath her gaze, his eyes lowering.

"There is a tale told among mortals of soul mates. Quite charming really, one I still laugh at." Selene smiled and held a hand out to Bede. "Long ago, when men were young, men and women were once made together. They shared a body, a heart, a soul. Then one day they were ripped apart, cast away from each other with the wind. Since that day, they seek to find their other half. Only their soulmate can ease the longing, the need burning so hotly beneath the surface."

"She is not of us."

"She will remain!" The ground beneath their feet trembled with the force of her displeasure. "If you wish to keep Saltar prisoner, wish to retain the freedom you have so blissfully enjoyed, you will listen to my words and heed them. Those who were forsaken will rise into the ranks. Among them, there are key holders, men and women with gifts. To cast them out is to risk his rising."

"If he rises, he will kill everyone." Bede stepped forward. "I had a dream of the carnage his rebirth would bring."

"Aye." Selene nodded. "You did not know at the time what it would mean. Hemat will bristle and growl, but he will accept you."

Bede glanced at Hemat who glowered at her. She shivered at the controlled hatred in his gaze and turned away. Snuggling deeper into Gawain's arms, she tried to forget the banked violence in his king's eyes. She took a deep breath. "It matters little to me, Goddess, if he does or not. My place is with my mate. I care nothing for anything beyond that."

"Of course I shall accept her." Hema snorted. "Do I look a fool to you? I asked what manner of creature she was...not ordered her death!"

Selene winked at Bede. "Good. I shall leave you to this. I have issue with a young god who has forgotten his manners." In a cloud of smoke, she vanished, leaving the stunned silence of the room.

"Milord, surely you don't think we must follow her order. We cannot risk all of our kind for the sake of that thing." Dorstan waved a hand at Bede.

"We shall do as she bids. War is on the horizon, Dorstan. Look beneath your feet, the floor still bears the scars of a recent battle, those are not false images."

Bede gasped as Gawain tugged her around the assembled warriors. She noted some were carrying wounded from the room, others were bundling the dead. Her eyes caught Ashalia's. The young girl smiled, bowed her head, and darted off after the queen who strode regally from the room.

"Milord, may I remind you what happened when you allowed a stranger to..." Dorstan's voice faded as Gawain tugged Bede into a room and closed the door.

A moment later her back slammed against the cold wood, his hot body pressed against hers. She shuddered at the heat in his gaze, his hands blocking her in as they pressed against the door on either side of her head.

"Milord?"

"I missed you." Gawain licked at her jaw. "I longed to see you, to touch you. I dreamed of you in pain and could do nothing."

"It doesn't matter now, milord. We're together now."

"Aye."

Bede whimpered as his lips descended on hers with bruising intent. Wrapping her arms around his shoulders, she squeezed, content to remain in his arms even if their fate was far from certain.

Desire flared, scorching along her skin with each brush of his hands. His fingers plucked the heavy armor from her shoulders and arms to clatter to the ground. Muffled giggles and harsh, uneven breathing filled the silence. Her body arched, pressing closer to him as he ground against her. The feel of his hard shaft teased her. She jumped with the first brush of his fingers against the swollen folds of her sex. A cold breath against her flesh before it faded to be replaced with heat, his fingers gliding through the moist proof of her lust.

Bede whimpered. Swallowing her moans, she clawed at his back, her eyes closing at the sensations flooding her body. Hot, wet, his mouth suckled at her nipple, his fangs scratching over the flesh, sending shards of pleasure straight to her groin.

A furious snarl from Gawain drew her attention. Tensing, she clung to him, her body swamped in a pleasurable haze. "Gawain?"

"Shh." Gawain inhaled. "Do you smell it?"

Bede inhaled, the rich smell of earth flooded the room. She frowned, her gaze sweeping the shadows. The sound of wings pulsed like a heartbeat, stirring the smell of water and earth to life. Her hand wrapped around Gawain's arm when he turned, his hand reaching for his weapon.

"What is it?" Bede's voice cracked, fear replacing any hint of arousal.

"I am uncertain." Gawain pressed her back against the door. "Stay behind me."

"I think not, milord. I am…"

"Now is not the time to question me."

"At ease, vampire. I mean no harm to you or your mate." The accented voice rose, filling the room before a figure appeared. A black crow's head flowed down into powerful shoulders covered only by a single, wide leather band.

"What are you?" Bede's fingers tightened until they ached.

"Khnum." Gawain shrugged.

"What?" She leaned forward, her chin on Gawain's shoulder. "What is it?"

"Khnum, he's the Egyptian god of…"

"It matters not, Bede. I bring a message to ease the burden in both your hearts." The mighty god settled on the edge of a cluttered altar. "'Tis rare to be so well thought of by Selene. Indeed, she barely glances at a mortal. You, however, are not a mortal anymore." He shifted his weight carefully. "Put your desire, your hunt for your sister to rest, for now, young one. Her destiny lies within the arms of Liam, within the safe embrace of her soul mate and not this world. Amuliana has drawn her into service, and if you were to rip her from it it would cause great harm to her. Take heart, Bede, she will be safe, protected, and loved until she finds her way to you."

"She is but a child, she deserves—"

"It must be this way." Khnum's feathers flared, his eyes flashing. "For victory to be within grasp we must follow the dictates. No harm will befall her. Una is under my protection and under the watchful gaze of my family. Amuliana will not dare to harm her."

"Milady? Bede?" Ashalia's voice drifted through the door. "Forgive my intrusion, but you and Lord Gawain have been summoned to stand before the king and his queens."

"Go." Khnum's form shifted, grains of sand falling from him to pool at his feet. "I shall keep Una safe."

A lone tear tracked down Bede's face as she stared at his vanishing form. A moment later, she pressed against Gawain, sobs shaking her frame. "My poor Una."

"Shh, my love," Gawain soothed. "I will find her, no matter how long it takes, nor what the cost. I swear it to you."

Bede nodded. His word would not be broken. Honor would dictate it could not, but what would the cost be to them for his search? Pain lanced through her. She couldn't stand the thought of losing him.

Tensing at the tender voice whispering at the back of her mind, she clung to her lover. "*Be happy, Bede. Embrace your future and fear not for me. I will find you when it is time.*" Her uncertainty and fear melted away with the realization that Una was safe—Khnum would protect her until Una found her mate and her freedom.

"Mistress?"

"We come now," Gawain barked out. "Come, my love, dry your eyes. We will meet this challenge before I renew my search."

"Nay," Bede gasped, her eyes widening. "Nay, we cannot, 'tis not right."

"We must stand before—"

"Nay, I mean we cannot continue to seek her so desperately. Una is safe, she is whole. When the time comes, she will return to me." Reaching up, she cupped his jaw. "She knew, I see that now. Always she saw so deeply within me, easing my fears. Even the night she was taken she soothed me. The gods have decided. I will seek her, but it must not consume us."

"If I had not failed you before..."

Bede shook her head. "You did not fail me. I didn't believe before, but I see now. Marshante was right. Una and I's paths were not meant to travel together. Our time will come, our connection cannot be broken by distance or time. Now come, we must stand before your king and we shall stand together. United."

Ignoring the ache in her heart, Bede wiped at her tears and rested her palms over his chest. Pasting a smile on her face, she took his hand and reached for the door handle.

She squeaked a protest when he jerked her into

his body. He pressed a hard kiss to her lips. "Together, it will be," he promised and reached over to open the door. With a squeeze of her hand, he led the way into the gathering light of the throne room.

Chapter Twenty-Four

Hemat stared at the pair before him. Rumpled, stained, they clung to each other. Gawain's fierce glower was an all too familiar expression, one Hemat knew would not be soothed with words. His sword dangled from his belt, the bloody blade within reach should he need it.

Beside him, her shift stained and torn, Bede glared. Her fingers flexing on the hilt of her dagger, a most impressive weapon. Indeed, it appeared the girl herself was a weapon. One meant to be wielded against Saltar...

A sharp jab in the ribs drew his attention to his queen. She stared pointedly at him, the raised eyebrow a clear warning. Throwing her a glower, Hemat shifted on his throne and cleared his throat.

"It appears we, the entire nation, owe you a debt of gratitude. Had you not brought your female to us, Gawain, victory may have been forfeit to us." The words burned like acid in his mouth and he swallowed hard.

"Hemat." Bruja's low voice left little room for doubt she'd honor her threat.

With a sigh, he nodded slightly. He knew she didn't trust him, but he would honor his word to his wives. Facing Gawain and Bede, he leaned forward.

"I did not bring Bede here to aid your war." Gawain's voice oozed disgust. "I brought her here to be safe from a threat in her world. It was the least of two evils at the time, but clearly, she is not any safer here, among her own people, than she was among the humans."

"Tell me, did you think we, as a vampire nation, would allow a mortal to wander about our cities unimpeded? We have no use for mortals. They are too weak to fuck and too weak to drink from." Dorstan ground out. "Our beloved king ordered you to bring to him one who could aid him. Instead, you dared to return with the bitch when you should have killed her and tracked down the whelp."

"Una is hardly a whelp." Bede whirled to face the threat. Her voice rang out over the room, a thread of steel within it. There was no hesitation in the woman, no back down at all. A formidable enemy to be had. Hemat swallowed his horrified gasp as her tunic slipped, revealing the spread wings of a bird rising from a pool. He shook himself as her voice rose in strength and fury. "She is my sister and worthy of protection. Neither she, nor I have done anything to you, except exist. Her loyalty to me, and mine to her, is beyond your understanding, it appears. Lizard drinker."

"Enough!" Hemat commanded, rising to his

feet. "Dorstan, she is of no concern to you. Keep to your mistresses and let those of us with more sense than to challenge our most impressive ally, defend this court. Gawain, I would ask your female if she can speak of it..."

"Speak of what?" Her eyes narrowed, back straightening.

"Gawain—"

"Her name is Bede." Gawain flashed his teeth, his eyes darkening with emotion. "And if you wish to speak to her, she's right there. Ask your questions or not. Either way, Bede is capable of speaking for herself. To ask me to speak for her is to disrespect both her and I."

"Do not defy me so blatantly, Gawain. I am still king."

"Bede, perhaps you would be kind enough to explain how you came to be here," Bruja interrupted. "There seems to be some confusion on behalf of our king. It is rare to have a mortal traverse through a gateway."

"I came with Gawain." Bede shrugged indifferently. "Marshante warned of a danger so we fled her home. That warning was only reinforced when we intercepted a warrior. It is here I am meant to be."

"Falsehoods!" Dorstan shouted. "You're here as

his whore and nothing—"

Gawain moved in a blur, his hand coming up to grab the other man's throat. His human form altered, fangs dripping, claws sharpened, body vibrating with the force of his fury.

"Mind your tongue, *lacerta drinkg*. Else I'd be tempted to slice it from your head."

Hemat growled, his temper fraying. Dorstan was a fool - it was the only explanation for insulting a newly mated vampire. He stomped down the steps from his dais and paused at the slow gurgling of Dorstan's breath as Gawain's fist tightened around his throat.

"Gawain, you will explain why you would dare to bring a mortal into our realm." Hemat strode forward. "Leave him and answer me."

"Because it was the only option."

"She is no more than food." Hemat shifted, unease fluttering at the disgust and fury in Gawain's eyes. "We do not bed our—"

"She is *mine*. We have spoken of this several times, Hemat. Yet you insist upon insulting both Bede and myself. I will not tolerate any further insults." Gawain's furious roar filled the hall. "You dare to speak of such a thing to me. Dare to insinuate I would not know my own soul. Of anyone in this room, King, you alone know what it means to lose your mated one."

Gawain's barb sank deep, ripping at a wound that still festered. Fury rose with his grief, lashing at him. Stepping back, he glanced at the woman Gawain had returned with and inhaled. His beloved Muandy had died for the lust of another. Centuries later he still felt the ache, the emptiness of her departure. It was not a feeling he'd wish on anyone.

"Mated does not mean loved." Hemat met Gawain's stare, awareness and acceptance within his heart. Some who were fated found their hearts tied to another lover, a sad state of affairs leading too often into isolation and destruction. Their kind was mated for a reason—and only those truly unlucky found mates belonging to another.

"She was loved long before she was mated," Gawain retorted.

Hemat nodded, his steps sure as he approached Bede. Stopping before her, he let himself smile as she met his stare head on. There didn't appear to be any fear within the young woman. "Tell me, Bede, do you truly understand what we are?"

"Hemat, do not question—"

"Be silent, Bruja. She must know the truth or she'll not survive."

"Are you asking if I know you are vampires?

Drinkers of blood? Demons who haunt the dreams of mortals?" Bede shook her head. "Beneath the pale flesh beats a heart pumping blood through each vein. I smell the heady scent, milord, and if I were truly ravenous, let me assure you, I would drink without guilt. If I were hungry enough, I would drink of you, one so important to his people. Indeed, your majesty, I am aware of what and who I am. I am Gawain's in body, heart, and soul."

Hemat nodded, hiding his inner glee. She knew, and had unwittingly given him a means to save face as well as keep the doors to his wives' chambers open to him. Of course he couldn't be so abrupt in his judgment, his people would question and connive for many years if he did too sudden an about-face. No, he would let things simmer for a bit longer. The girl could not go about challenging a king without there being consequences.

Turning, he strode back to his throne to settle. "Call forth Veronique du Coudray, there will be a wedding this eve."

"Milord, I must…"

Hemat met Dorstan's furious gaze. "As my captain it is your duty to escort Gawain to his marital bed. I trust you find no displeasure in this task?"

"Majesty, I beg off the task." Dorstan bowed. "Selordan will assist him in the putting to bed. It is beneath me to assist in the weakening of our bloodlines by allowing mortals to walk among us."

Murmurs of shock rose around the chamber as the captain stormed from the room, his fury making him stiff. Looking at his wife, Hemat raised a brow. He would have to deal with Dorstan and those loyal to his Captain. In time. Now, he had ruffled feathers to deal with.

"Leave him. If he wishes to turn from his sacred duty it is upon his soul." Bruja rose, her gown shimmering in the flickering torch light. "My sisters and I will escort Bede to the temple. Ashalia, see the chamber is prepared. Selordan, you'll assist Gawain to the temple."

"As you wish, milady." Selordan took Gawain's arm, tugging him from the room.

Hemat watched Bede appraise the room, her chin lifting slightly before she followed Bruja and his other wives from the room. Slinking down in his throne, he smothered a groan. A wedding after a battle was a most awkward method, but he could find no discontent within it. Rather, the rushing would soothe those who dared to question him and his acceptance. What better way to secure the greatest weapon they had but to bring her into the folds of his nation?

Chapter Twenty-Five

The shadows stretched across the floor as Bede stepped through the massive doors. Standing in the glow of candles, numerous women in long, flowing scarlet and black gowns stared at her. Each was drapped in elaborate jewels, as if their rank within the realm were of greatest of importance.

Bede clenched her fists at her sides and half turned to the door where Ashalia and Bruja hovered. "I don't know what–"

"Come, let us get you clean. Battle is never pleasant, and you have done us a great service today, Bede." Bruja slipped the stained shift from her shoulders and eased her toward the steaming tub in the center of the room. "We are honored to welcome one of your line back into our fold." She poured a sweet-smelling liquid into the water and waved two delicate-looking girls forward. "It has been too long our lord has suffered, too long he has punished the innocent."

He deserved to suffer for his sins. Punishing the innocent hardly endeared him to her. His treatment of her was enough to turn her stomach. "The innocent are so easily punished, aren't they?" Bede raised a brow. "Cast aside, used for another's purpose. It is as if they are mere pawns in life."

"Hemat's punishment was severe but his grief–"

"I believe those who are guilty should pay the penance for their actions." Bede stepped away from the steaming bath. "You are all wives of Hemat, loyal to him?"

"Indeed." Bruja picked up a silver chalice. "We are all wives, sisters. He has taken many wives to hide the loss of one."

"I am certain he grieves." Bede dipped her fingers in the water. The hot water tingled across her skin, the steam rising rich with the aroma of flowers and spice. "I grieve for my mother, my sister. It rips at my heart, and yet, I have not condemned an entire race for their loss."

"No? You blame the humans for the loss of your mother."

"I blame my father and uncle. It is upon their shoulders her death rests. Not upon the entire race." Bede exhaled. "Even now, your king permits me to remain because it suits him. Should his thoughts turn I have little doubt he would allow me to live."

"You hold no loyalty to our lord?"

"I hold loyalty to one. My husband. His loyalty to your king stands."

"Hemat will not be pleased to hear such things. He is fierce in his demand for loyalty of his people."

"Hemat's opinion holds no value to me." Bede smiled and stepped into the tub. "Keep your loyalty, I will keep mine. Now, tell me of the war and the reason Gawain wears a mask of guilt, of failure."

The women clustered around whispered to themselves as if her words had burned them. Bruja held up a hand, halting the conversation. "Sisters, enough. Hemat demands loyalty, yet has not proved himself to her. He blames himself for something which was not his doing." Bruja settled into a tall-backed chair. "Four hundred years ago, on a night such as this, we were rejoicing. The red moon is a period for all vampires to celebrate. A rebirth of our kind, if you will. That night was no different, our warriors were victorious on the battlefield, and our queen was entering a fertile cycle. Then Saltar came. With his seeming service to Hema the guards did not feel they needed to watch over him. How wrong they were. Gawain broke the door down to reveal Saltar standing with our queen's neck beneath his lips, blood everywhere. He had ripped her throat out—drank of one of our own."

"How did my kind become?"

"Hemat punished all who served Saltar, even those who he had enslaved. It mattered not, Hemat cursed them all. Cast them out into the mortal world, forgotten by our kind. Took away the gifts Selene granted us and discarded them all in his grief."

"He stole something given by Selene? A fearless man - or mad."

"Hemat is a little of both, I think."

"Now that Saltar is rising, the transgressions are overlooked." Bede drew a lazy circle in the water. "He craves revenge."

"Yes, but his bonds are not controlled by one key. Naw, there are several of them. A key for the species he condemned—vampire, dragon, fae, demon, and ankoù. He has inflicted much pain and little reward. Death would be too welcome for him. In his own small way, Gawain blames himself for Saltar's treachery."

The truth behind the words settled like a heavy weight around Bede's neck. Huffing a breath, Bede bit her lip. What if this wasn't real? What if all of this was just another dream? Something to keep her warm at night? Pulling her knees to her chest, she stared down into the water. What if in her Gawain had found someone who could help him forget his shortcomings, his failures?

"Did you know the warriors of Gawain's line take an oath?" Bruja raised her glass. "They swear on their honor not to indulge in the temptation of the flesh. Gawain, unlike many of his brethren, has never shown any interest in the immoral relations so many of our young men take part in."

"Perhaps he just—"

"Hadn't found you yet." Bruja glanced at her sisters, a smile on her face. "You were loved before you were claimed, Bede. 'Tis the way of the House of Serpents. His sect, his clan have always honored their vows. It is what makes them so dangerous."

"Any my clan?"

The gathered women exchanged glances and laughed. "You, my dear, are far more dangerous than any I have ever known. You, Bede, hold the power of the moon in your hands." Bruja straightened. "Enough of this melancholy. Let us discuss your wedding. Would you prefer gold?"

"Um, whatever you say, majesty," Bede acquiesced. "I'm not particular in my attire."

Bruja grinned and clapped her hands. "'Tis not a mortal wedding you're attending, my dear girl. You will be painted with the gold after you're bathed. Vanex, see we have the sugars ready."

"Sugars?"

"Indeed, I am well-versed with the culture you lived in. The sugars are to help keep you clean. 'Tis a fact, all young Roman women prefer to be without hair. Until they are wed, of course."

Bede flushed. She'd heard the tales of Roman women's extraordinary methods of grooming. Her fingers patted her hair, the very idea of pulling it out was beyond comprehension. A faint noise drew her attention to the tall, thin Vanex who laid out several long robes, a small container of bubbling liquid sat beside it, wrapped in simple strips of fabric.

"Come, milady."

Rising from the warmth of the bath, Bede smiled her appreciation at the young girl who held her wrap. Tugging the woolen material up around her shoulders, Bede followed the gentle nudge of Vanex at her back.

"'Tis okay, lay down. We'll be as quick as can be," Vanex soothed.

"Why do I take no comfort from your words?" Stretching out on the bed, Bede glanced at Bruja who smiled indulgently before slipping from the room. Sucking in a quick breath, Bede's eyes flew to Vanex at the hot swipe of something along her flank.

"Take a deep breath, milady, and we'll be done in a few moments."

Vanex's words did little to soothe her unease. Rather, she wondered if the other woman really hated her. Jumping at Vanex's careful touch, Bede clenched her fingers into the robes and inhaled. "Are you quite certain this is necessary?" Bede grabbed her wrist.

"Of course." Vanex smiled. "We do keep abreast of mortal customs. Your people have been doing this for a number of years. Is it not considered fashionable?"

"Fashionable?" Bede sucked in a quick, pained breath as the strip of fabric was ripped off her flesh. "How can it be fashionable to torture yourself? You ripped the hair out. Goodness, I am sure I'll bleed to death before you're finished."

"There's no blood. It'll grow back." Vanex frowned. "Until you grow into your immortal being, then it won't. Really, I am quite good at it. I used to serve a very wealthy Roman woman who thought nothing of having this done on a weekly basis."

"Yeah, well, no one ever said their women were smart," Bede ground out as Vanex finished sugaring the other flank. "And Gawain never complained before."

"Men, they never do." Vanex smoothed rose-scented oil down her hip, rubbing it into the sensitive flesh of her thighs, dipping between her legs. "Besides, Gawain wouldn't complain, not after eight hundred years of abstinence."

Bruja slipped back into the room, a chalice in her hand. "Abstinence? Selene, one would have had to have sex before they can truly abstain. He joined the order at a delicate age before his right of passage. For all his faults, his blustering, he was no wandering vampire." Bruja giggled softly. "I think it incredibly romantic, you and he are your only lovers. I don't see either of you breaking the vows and taking a lover. Unless you're both into it."

"Bruja! Be still your tongue. She's all but a virgin, freshly plucked." Vanex swatted at her before dipping a wide brush into the carved bowl near Bede's head. "Though I wonder if Selordan will ensure he's truly prepared. The boy hasn't had but one lover."

"Vanex! Please, keep on track. It matters not if Gawain's prepared. He is past his immortal birth, the tattoos will be mark enough. Now, make haste, the bells toll."

Bede tilted her head, the faint sound of bells growing louder. "What is it? Are we…"

"No, the priestess has arrived," Vanex explained. "Come now, we must get you dressed."

"Dressed?" Bede winced at the thought.

"Indeed." Bruja waved aside one of the younger girls and wrapped a narrow gold and black rope

271

around her hips, knotting it so the end dangled down between her legs. As Vanex trailed the brush across her throat, down her arms, she watched Bruja gather gold threads and braid them together into a narrow, delicate-looking rope. More than a little uneasy at the thought of having the queen helping her, she flinched at the cool touch along her throat.

"Relax, child." Bruja's soft voice was filled with humor. "Contrary to the devilish stories you've heard, my desire to aid you has nothing to do with the blood flowing through your veins and everything to do with a debt which has remained unpaid for centuries."

"A debt?"

Her eyes sad, Bruja nodded. "Perhaps I will tell you of it another time. Now, it is time for you to be wed. If you do so choose. You do not have to accept Gawain as your—"

"But he is." Bede squeezed her hand. "He is my other half, my soul mate. Perhaps I knew it all along. I realized it when I saw him fighting for me. He was the monster in my dreams. The one who came to save me from the life I had."

The other women in the room nodded. Fate was kinder to some than others.

Chapter Twenty-Six

Veronique du Coudray, high priestess of the Rouge Arianrhod, stepped through the ornate doors into King Hema of the Bloodseekers throne room. She assessed those assembled as she drifted along the marble floor to stand before the king. He'd aged in the years since Muandy's death, the vitality she'd long associated with him ebbing with each passing year. Still, he was king, and until his wives produced a clear heir, he would rule.

Though, there was one, who held the right to the throne he was not aware of. One would through blood could usurp him - if she chose to.

"My king."

"Priestess. You know why you have come."

Veronique raised a brow, her hands linked together. "Indeed, though I must admit it is uncommon to call for me to perform a common wedding. It is a chore better suited to one of my priestesses in training. Still, your male was quite insistent upon my attendance. Curious, I decided to honor his query in the spirit it was sent."

"I sent for you…" Hemat paused, fury crossing his face with the entrance of Dorstan, a warrior renowned for killing dragons and his stubborn will. "What is the meaning of your return? Have you changed—"

"I have not. I must voice my disagreement once more, milord. To allow this...this mortal to come to our realm and be so welcomed..."

"Bede is Gawain's mate, his other half. His bride by the Fates. Do you challenge Selene's wisdom?" Hemat ground out, his eyes flashing red.

"She is a female and as such less than rational."

"She is the Mother of all, Dorstan. To doubt her is to invite her wrath."

"She is a female. Her wrath is of no concern to me, my lord. Allowing Gawain's mortal bitch to remain is. Weak and frail she will fade beneath the weight of our world and leave him a broke shell. She must be destroyed–"

"He speaks of Gawain's intended?" Veronique eyed Dorstan. The man was driven by lust and greed. For him to hate a woman simply because another had claimed her was not uncommon. For him to argue with the king, however, was.

"She is from the mortal realm. Hardly of equal to any of our females. He would do better to take one of–"

"You speak of her with such disregard." Veronique offered a cold smile. "Is she not gifted by Selene? Blessed in this union?"

"Selene herself blessed her." Hemat started.

"I see. So you question not only your king, but your goddess." Veronique straightened. "You risk much, Dorstan, for so little gain. Bede's arrival heralds a new era for our people. The gods themselves have touched her. You hold no weight to their claim, Captain."

"She will weaken him."

"Weaken?" Veronique cast a glance around. Charred shadows remained on the floor, the remnants of a battle fought and won. "I would hate to see what she would do if she were to strengthen Gawain."

"Your concerns are noted, Dorstand. Return to your quarters."

"It will be your grave, milord," Dorstan warned before vanishing into a cloud of sulfuric smoke.

"I assume he is displeased with the choice of brides?"

"She is mortal. Newly claimed and not yet grown into her immortality." Hemat waved aside further questions. "You will honor us by wedding them."

Veronique inhaled slowly. Discontent and anger rolled through the crowd. Vampires from all clans had come together, be it in peace or not she was uncertain. The air was thick with the stench of death, smudges of soot clung to the cracks and breaks in the stone, and more than one vampire still bore evidence of a fresh battle.

"You honor me, on this eve of our holiest nights."

"They come." A voice rose from the corridors leading to the throne room.

The tall doors were swung open and several youngsters approached from each corridor. Veronique eyed the chalices, the ribbons, and glanced at the king. Whomever they were, their place within the palace was envious. Perhaps a son of one of the queens was to be married. More than one of Hema's wives had brought a child to the union. She swayed slightly at the woman who strode into the room, her body bare except for the paint and a delicate length of rope that hung around her hips. Her groin was neatly trimmed, the hair all but gone, tiny dots of blood dried on the pale skin. Her hair had been piled atop her head, golden threads woven through it.

Where had Hemat found her? The line long since broken, there were no instances of one within the hallowed halls for centuries. Nervously, she traced the pale lines of the girl's tattoos, noting the narrowed eyes of the serpent. Veronique swallowed, she understood much now. It would be no ordinary wedding—the king sought to appease the gods tonight by accepting one of Selene's chosen back into her rightful place.

Masking her shock, Veronique glanced at the other side of the room and sighed. The warrior striding toward her resembled a familiar man she'd long since mourned. At one time she'd have welcomed him into her bed, a rare honor bestowed on few, yet he'd never shown any inclination. Unlike those he surrounded himself with, he had kept to the old vows with unquestionable resolve. His dark hair was slicked back, eyes feverish with lust, he was focused solely on the woman the queen assisted until she knelt before her.

Veronique closed her eyes, focusing inward on the image of their goddess. The rustle of flesh beneath fabric filled her ears, yet she did not open her eyes. All must be focused on Selene's benevolence. Exhaling, she welcomed the rush of power, the insight into the pair. Beneath their calm exteriors, a warrior's heart beat in tandem. Love, unlike any she'd ever felt, flowed between them. Joined not only by the claiming but a force far greater, a thread unbreakable by even death, it stretched between them like a steel rope.

She swept the room with a final glance. The power of the red moon flowed through her, calling out to Selene, to the Fates in their wisdom as she began the incantations needed to breach the very heavens and rise around their goddess.

"Praise Selene, goddess of old, mother to us all, on this night. Tonight we welcome not only one of our kind into our midst, but we honor the wishes of our great and bountiful mother." Veronique lifted her palms to the ceiling. "Selene, we beg thee to honor this couple, to grant them forever in peace. We ask you to guide them to an eternal happiness so deserving."

With a smile she looked at the young couple before her, their eyes locked in silent communication. "The ties that bind you are stronger than any other. Fate has given your other half back. Honor this with kindness, truth, joy." Veronique ushered a serving boy forward. He dropped to a knee, the tray held above his bowed head. She lifted the intricately jeweled chalice from the tray. "Rise, Gawain and Bede. Rise and swear fealty to none but yourselves."

"Should I forsake you, may the sun greet me with a prolonged death." Gawain took the chalice and sipped from it before handing it to Bede. "In my blood I give of myself, of my life, and my heart. From my loins may I grace you with a daughter as beautiful as you, to warm your heart and light your soul with joy. In this, my beloved, I offer my solemn vow, bind me now as your love has freed me."

"Should I dishonor our vows, I will greet the

morning with a willing heart and a fitting death," Bede promised. "In my life I will give of my blood, of my womb, to you a life for eternity or until Paradise has called us to her feet. May I bless you with a son to carry your name, your line, and give to you a pride and honor your heart yearns for. Bind me now, milord, my love, as your love, your life, has freed me."

"So it shall be. In honor, in life do I bind thee." Veronique wove a length of gold rope around their hands before piercing their flesh with a dagger and holding the wounds together. "Only death shall keep thee apart until the end of time."

Glancing around, Veronique returned her attention to the couple, her smile warming. Their focus had not moved from the other, love and peace filled their eyes. Smiles of yearning and warmth lit their faces. "Selene will bless thee tonight. Ask for what you truly desire and it shall be yours."

Bede glanced at her before refocusing on Gawain, her bottom lip between her teeth. "I can ask for anything?"

"Anything so long as your heart is pure." Veronique wondered what she would ask for. Many asked for a healthy child or a day to walk in the sun. Would a mortal seek something beyond the grasp of all?

Bede leaned forward, her eyes sparkling as she pressed in closer. "I would prefer Vanex and her sugars never come together in my presence again."

Veronique frowned before following Bede's gaze down. Flushing, she chuckled, the tension bleeding from her shoulders at the words. Her heart was as pure as her soul, and in such innocence, such naivety, Gawain had been blessed beyond any other. "I think that is something Selene cannot give. Ask for anything beyond—"

"I have all I need." Bede shrugged, her eyes flashing with laughter and happiness. "My sister will return to me in time, my love is standing beside me for all eternity—what more could I seek?"

"A healthy heir? A day to walk among the living? The life of another? Ask it and you shall be granted any prize this eve."

Bede shook her head. "Gawain has given me all the blessings, all the prizes I could pray for, mistress. How can I tempt the gods by asking for more than the bounty I have been given? Love, life, a mate worthy of Selene herself, and freedom from the misery and deceit beneath my uncle's rule. I thank thee, but I have no prize I seek beyond the man who stands before me."

"And you, milord?"

Gawain offered a crooked smirk. "I have no desire for more. I am a soldier—we have no elaborate desires."

Hiding her pleasure proved taxing as she appraised the young couple. Veronique nodded and held the chalice up. "Drink of it again, united. I bless you both in the name of Selene, mother of all."

"Indeed, be blessed, my captain." Hemat's voice rose above the cheers. "Honor me with your service as I honor you and your bride with a gift befitting such unquestionable faith."

Veronique glanced at Bruja who eyed her husband with uncertainty as he strode from the throne to stand before Gawain and Bede. "Highness—"

"This night..." Hemat paused, his gaze sweeping the room, sorrow in his gaze. "I have long dreaded, long wallowed in the misery of the memories. Tonight, my dear Bede, wife to Gawain, I offer to you a place within my court. I also offer to you this."

Veronique gasped as an elaborate choker was brought forth, the blue and gold flickering and dancing in the moonlight. She stepped back, her fingers curling into fists at the sight of Maudhnait's gems. The fallen queen had worn them to her coronation, beautiful, exotic they'd been a gift from Hemat—for him to give them to the wife of a warrior was an honor few would dare to dream of.

"Milord." Bruja approached, her gaze on the stones. "You honor us all with such a gift. I would offer something as well, Bede."

"What do you have to offer?" Veronique shifted, fearful for the young couple settling like acid in her heart. Were they out to turn it into a competition? How would a mortal unused to the ways of vampire court react? "You honor Selene with your generosity, your benevolence."

There was nothing in Bruja's gaze that spoke of competition, of jealousy. Instead, a warmth settled around the queen like a blanket. "A simple gift." Bruja smiled her hand curling over Hemat's wrist. "My gift is not something one can see or touch. Instead, I would honor you by offering you a place within my ladies. Please, Bede, accept the place of your ancestors and join the ladies in waiting."

Veronique wondered if Bruja would be so generous if Bede refused her gift. Although it was an honor, it was not really a gift. To serve the queen was more work than any one woman could ever hope to avoid.

"Thank you, highness, but..." Bede glanced uneasily at Gawain. "I only wish to be with Gawain. I do not want more than I have, can you forgive me?"

Bruja laughed, her hand closing over Bede's. "Child, you honor me simply by being here. In you I see the joy and life return to one of my husband's most trusted guards. Go, enjoy your husband. Think about my gift, there is no rush."

"You are most kind."

"Let us proceed with the putting to bed." Veronique waved at the hovering crowd. "Then the rest of us can get to the feasting and party."

Chapter Twenty-Seven

Bede leaned against Gawain, her voice a whisper. "Why are there so many following us?"

Gawain glanced behind them, taking in the long train of men and women at their heels. The tradition was one he had often dreamed of, but never thought he'd experience. He met Bede's stare, a soft smile curling his lips. "'Tis customary for the putting to bed. Many human cultures have something similar as a symbol of the purity of the wedding bed. Our people use it for another reason."

"Oh." Bede frowned, confused. "What reason?"

"We do it to gauge how loud the party can get." Ashalia giggled as she swept open the bedroom door.

Bede stepped into the room, her eyes widening in horror. Surrounding the room, dressed in full military regalia, what seemed an entire legion of vampires held their swords aloft. In the middle of the room on a raised dais, a huge bed rested, the covers turned down. Scarlet sheets spilled onto the floor, and gauze curtains shrouded the bed. At the head, two massive guards stood, hands locked before their groins, legs spread.

Terror raced through Bede when Ashalia pulled her closer to the bed. Why would there be so many in the room? Surely they wouldn't all— Her racing thoughts were interrupted by the sensation of cool fingers removing her rope belt and the jewels decorating her throat and ears. Ashalia nudged her into sitting on the bed before lifting her feet one at a time and tucking her into the delicate bedding. Bede reached for the blankets only to grasp at thin air as Ashalia lifted them.

Turning to Gawain, she swallowed as the young upstart who'd pulled her from the battle assisted him into bed. Selordan repeated the same motions Ashalia had with care and precision. With Gawain laid out on the bed, Ashalia and the young warrior began the process of rolling the bedding down to the foot of the bed.

"Wait, we might…" Bede flushed, humiliated at so many seeing her naked body. Crossing one arm over her chest, she shielded her breasts and cupped her groin to hide what lay between her legs. "Please, just leave them."

"Milady." Ashalia smiled. "'Tis your wedding night. I hardly think you'll be in need of bedclothes. The fire has been stoked. If you have need of refreshments, there's a fine wine right here. We bid you good eve." She bowed, clapped her hands, and wiggled her fingers at the male guards who began marching out the door.

Bede squirmed closer to Gawain, determined not to panic in the face of such an unusual happenstance. She gasped when Ashalia closed the chamber door and locked it…with her and Selordan on the inside. "Uh, wait I thought…"

"As per our duties…" Selordan bowed, his eyes carefully averted. "We cannot leave until the marriage has been…"

"If you say 'consummated', I will rise from this bed and—"

"'Tis hard to see bloodstains on red." Ashalia flushed.

"But we've already had relations," Bede sputtered, her face on fire.

"Our duties are clear, to shirk them—"

"For the love of all that is unholy," Gawain roared. "Get out before I use you for a scabbard."

Bede nodded feverishly. "Forgive me for my bluntness, but you can leave. We've no need for you to be here."

"But Bruja—"

"Go." Gawain's low growl filled the room.

With a quick nod, Selordan and Ashalia teleported out of the room. Alone, the butterflies began dancing in Bede's belly, waltzing with her arousal until she couldn't say where one started and another stopped. Nervous, she plucked at the sheet beneath her. "Milord…"

"Gods above, I thought I'd lost you." Gawain pressed a hot kiss to her throat, his tongue darting over her skin. "That it would never come to be. My nights were haunted by fear, nd the belief I was beyond your forgiveness."

"Milord, my love, you have not failed me." Bede swallowed against the burning in her eyes. "I only hope to win your love one day."

"You hold my heart in your hands, my love." Gawain pinned her to the bed, his thigh between hers, his hand holding both of her wrists above her head. "I swear, my love, if there is one thing I desire more than any other it is your love. Forever, I would hold your heart safe."

Tears streaming down her face, Bede wiggled her hips against his. "I do love you. Long ago I stopped worrying about Una, instead I worried about you. I prayed for your safety, wanted to have you in my life, arms, and bed. I gladly embrace this world, this life, to be with you."

Bede moaned at the soft brush of his lips. She licked her lips, catching his, the sweetness of the wine lingering on her tongue. Giggling softly, she struggled within his grasp until he let go. Encircling his neck with her arms, she clung to him.

"I will make everything work for us, my love. I promise, I shall return your sister to you and make your family whole." Gawain pressed a kiss to her shoulder, his mind wandering for a heartbeat. He still owed the gatekeeper the sand. When he returned to Amuliana's realm he'd need to remember to pick up the sands he owed. Perhaps it would suffice as enough of an excuse to keep his beloved from worrying when he went to hunt again.

"Milord, I know well you desire to do so, but it will come to be in time." Bede arched her hips. "So, my lover, shall we put aside our discussion? 'Tis been so long since I've felt you within me." She trailed her palm down his chest, her nails scoring the flesh until she could grasp his hard cock. Slowly, she pumped him, her grip tightening with each downward stroke.

"Ah, my first task is to please." Gawain groaned, his hips lurching forward. "It shall be done."

Chapter Twenty-Eight

Selene stepped past the guard, her gaze searching the shadows. Movement caught her eye and the figure of a man with a bird's head appeared. A smile lifted one corner of her mouth. "The wedding was splendid. Glorious in all its naked glory. The bride was ravishing, the groom looking eager for the ravishment. Hemat bestowed a most impressive gift on young Bede. Bede barely glanced at the jewels, I don't believe there is any love loss there. Queen Bruja offered her a much coveted place within her ranks, and as anticipated, Bede turned her down. I fear the royals will find Bede a little less in awe of them they would like." She helped herself to a glass of wine. "I did not see you in attendance. Well, honestly, I dare say I saw no other gods there, which saddens me."

"I had other, more pressing issues." Khnum set aside the clay figure he was working on. "I had a thought - what would I gift them for their wedding. After much debate, I've put a blessing on them. Thankfully, Amuliana didn't appear. She'd have ruined the entire ceremony."

"I'm certain she would have, save for her attendance within the dragon's realm. It was my understanding she was busy within the sheets of some dragon lord's bed. Knowing the heart of young Bede, I attended Una rather than the wedding."

Selene nodded, all too aware of her old friend's activities. "You were eager to visit a pair of young lovers before the ceremony. They certainly are not shy in the pleasure they take from each other's body."

"I wanted to ease her fears. She's so brave, her heart is pure, youthful. I could do no less."

"It will be rewarded," Selene promised. "You have eased her mind and now I will ask you to guard young Una, for her fate lies with one many have already forsaken. Liam is a man who fears his chains—he has no awareness of just how closely his life is tied to the woman that Una will come to be."

"His mind is consumed with his quest at the moment, but in time he will know. The day he sees her, his quest will become a vague memory he clings to as his heart opens to the love he is deserving of."

"What do you think will be done about them? Do you think there will be something we can take before the council?"

"You know as well as I *she* has plans. I hold no hope they are decent, honest ones. She will use

Una to suit her needs and when the girl is of no further use, or she cannot control her power any longer, she will attempt to destroy her."

"Yes."

"How sweet. If it isn't the walking dead and the bird brain."

Selene rolled her eyes and turned. "Amuliana, what an unpleasant intrusion." Repulsion dripped like acid from her words. She stepped closer to the light, her gaze never straying from the figure strolling toward her.

"I'm sure." Tugging her silver gown tighter around her, Amuliana sashayed into the room. Her eyes swept the shadows, a cunning in them that drew a sneer from Selene. "So she survived long enough to wed. How quaint. An immortal passing as a mortal passing as an immortal. Enough to give even the most stalwart of us a headache, wouldn't you agree?"

"Was there something you desired? Some man who's cock you wish to ride?"

"I simply desired to attend so I could give them a wedding gift, but sadly, I was unable to." Amuliana sneered. "A mystical block I think." Any façade of friendship dropped much like the mask she wore. Dark shadows flickered over her face, gaunt cheeks twitched. The ugly soul within the shell flickered before she masked it with care.

"If you'd like to leave your gift with me, I'll make sure they get it." Selene held out a hand. "Oh, but I forgot, your gifts usually precede something terrible and haggard. So what evil do you wish to part with today?"

"My gifts are not to be toyed with." Amuliana snickered. "My gifts are as lavish as my affections."

"Perhaps, both are deadly. You are not welcome within my chambers, Amuliana. I've no desire to share my bed with you."

"Indeed, there is no fool's bed to slither in, no men to seduce and manipulate here." Selene stepped closer. Fury danced beneath her skin, the urge to slap her nemesis' face strong. Restraining herself, Selene glanced at the other god before focusing on Amuliana, her fingers pressed into Amuliana's chest, her nails cutting into the flesh. "Mark my words, harlot, there will come a time when your lack of decency shall be your downfall."

"Your petty jealousy makes you rather reckless. After all, if one is in bed with those with the power, they have control. Men are easy to manage, they do their thinking with what's between their legs rather than between the ears. Control that and you control him. A tidbit to remember, my dearest. One should always keep an eye on the prize." Amuliana waved a hand in the air, a hurt manner about her as she turned away.

Selene spat a curse as Amuliana vanished into the night. Who would be next to fall prey to Amuliana and her lust. Barely acknowledging her friend's nod, Selene stalked from the room. Bede was safe for now, but who else would be destroyed before Amuliana and her cur of a lover were contained forever?

Author Note

Thank you for reading His Blooded Mate, if you enjoyed Gawain and Bede's story, please consider leaving a review.

Join my biweekly Newsletter and get inside information, access to updates, and much more.

~*~

A Demon's Curse

Dank stone walls rose high above him as Angrail entered the great hall of Nepharal, God of the Underworld. Demons filled the room, their boisterous voices rose in laughter. Some called out to him, others jeered as he passed. Angrail snatched his cloak away from one young upstart who got too close, his tattoos glowing an eerie pink. Pathetic, barely grown into his station. He bared his teeth but did not linger.

He strode up to the raised dais, the throne carved of rock and bone was occupied by a figure shrouded in endless robes. Sparks skittered across the dark folds, smoke and cinder rising up with each breath. Angrail stopped at the bottom of the steps, and stared at the Lord of the Dead.

"You dare to presume you are above my judgment!" Flames leapt and rocks crumbled around the throne room as Nepharal, Keeper of the Dead, roared his displeasure.

Angrail braced himself in the face of his master's fury. How dare the god berate him? As if he were wrong, when justice should have been sought for those slaughtered. "No, I don't presume anything, Lord of the Dead. One cannot feel fear or anything really in the face of such disregard."

"You forget your place, Angrail."

"No, I do not. I feel no remorse for what I have done. Justice will be served. You would not act! They have committed the ultimate of sins, taken—"

"I am aware of the crimes, Angrail. It seems you have forgotten you are not the judge, jury, and executioner. I will give the orders, for those such as you, who are servants of my order. There is a reason I have my huntresses, and it is not for you to—"

"Your order? No, Nepharal, I am not a servant of your order. I am a Myst, a guide of the light, of paradises. One who should never have had to bear such a burden. You do not command me, Lord of the Dead. Your wife does."

"My wife is well aware of your actions, Angrail. She has wept for your fall. By taking justice into your hands, you have fallen from her ranks. You, Angrail, are of my order now."

"I will never be one of your hunters. They are too busy with their revelry and seeking their next fuck to care about such things as the honor of women, children, who have been slaughtered. You say it is for them to hunt those responsible for the misery of others? Then why do I see none of them going after those who were party to the brutality, my lord?" Angrail waved a hand at the demonesses standing guard next to the throne. "Instead, they stand about your throne room, flaunting their attributes, and leave the task to others."

"You dare to challenge my warriors?" Horns flaring, a demoness stepped forward, claws and fangs lengthening. Her skin darkened and the intricate markings stood out in stark relief.

"Silence, Lemraya." Nepharal waved a gnarled hand at her, sending her back into line. "I will deal with Saltar and his followers in due time, Angrail. Justice is not always quick. Sometimes it can take time. Show remorse for your actions and I will grant you a boon."

~*~

About the Author

Elise Whyles is a Canadian Paranormal Romance Author. Combining her love of mythology, romance, and adventure, Elise brings each aspect to life in her work.

She lives on the prairies with her family, and their group of eccentric fur babies. She is an avid reader and loves to garden and crochet. For more information about her, you can check out her website. https://sultryreads.com/elise-whyles/

www.ingramcontent.com/pod-product-compliance
Lightning Source LLC
Chambersburg PA
CBHW030645020726
47493CB00006B/1879